Otter Creek 1936

Life in the Foothills of the St. Francois Mountains

RITA BECK

outskirts
press

Outskirts Press, Inc.
http://www.outskirtspress.com

ISBN: 978-1-9772-1022-7

Cover Image by Rita Beck

Outskirts Press and the "OP" logo are trademarks belonging to Outskirts Press, Inc.

PRINTED IN THE UNITED STATES OF AMERICA

This book is dedicated to Mont and Golda Jordan Black, my maternal Grandparents. They raised five children during the difficult days of the Great Depression. They instilled in their children the values of hard work, education and prayer in those dark days of economic uncertainty. Their community relied on neighbor helping neighbor and a deep faith in God to meet their daily needs.

Acknowledgements

Thank you to Albert Campbell for his help with the technical advice and his knowledge of molasses making, pigs and mules and editing the finished product. Thanks to Joe Politte for his art work and his wife Geraldine for her support. Thanks to my Grandmother Lillian Beck for her love of storytellling. Also to Lowell Goggin, who on a summer afternoon shared a story of a lazy mule.

Ottery Creek 1936

THE DEPRESSION FOUND us, my Mother, Father, Brother Bill and Sister Grace and me, living on a hillside farm in the foot hills of the St Francois Mountains, in the Missouri Ozarks. Our farm stretched along a rambling stream called Ottery Creek. Cambrian age bed rock lined the creek bed, keeping the spring fed waters of Ottery Creek crystal clear. Bluffs rose sharply on the far-side of the sparkling water of the creek. Hickory and oak forest, with a smattering of maple and sumac and dogwood thrown in, blanketed the west side of the creek, rising and falling into steep ravines and ridges, broken only by a patchwork of small farmsteads, an occasional country store or a little white frame church house, stretched all the way to Salem, Missouri.

Up the creek a ways, was a valley with a narrow, gravel road winding through it. The ribbon of a road crossed Ottery Creek and traveled up the hill to the cemetery where the Ottery Creek people laid their loved ones to rest. A wagon, draped in black, drawn by a team of mules or work horses, would wind along the gravel road, carrying the body of a loved one resting in the bed of the wagon. People dressed in mourning clothes would be walking or riding in buggies behind the wagon. The harmony of the people of Ottery would ring through the valley as they sang *Amazing Grace* or *The Old Rugged Cross* as the procession meandered up the gravel road.

If you had surveyed the hillsides surrounding our valley, you would have wondered how we survived in that rocky environment. You would have also noted the beauty and wondered how anyone could have borne to leave those hills. Our little forty acre farm lay alongside the stream, from one crossing of Ottery to the other crossing, or *ford* as people in rural Missouri called the shallow areas where the rivers and creeks could be crossed. The people of Ottery had lived along that creek since the American Settlers came into the valley in the 1830's.

On one bluff, rising from Ottery Creek were the words, *mined for gold in 1842, carved on the face of the rock.* How often I wondered about the unknown man who had taken his time to tell of his efforts to find wealth in that creek and boulders that bordered it. Was he a wild eyed hermit, with bushy hair, driven with a crazed lust for gold, wandering the hills and rivers, living off the land? Did something hold him to this valley, not permitting him to wander farther west in search of gold during the gold rush of 1849, binding him to these hills and valleys, forever searching for gold? Or did he join the westward miners? We will probably never know who the man was.

Brother, Sister and I loved to climb on that bluff and run our hands over the carving. Maybe there was gold in that bluff or in the spring fed waters of Ottery Creek! We would wade in the cool water on hot summer days, turning over rocks, dreaming of finding gold. On occasions, Sister, Brother or I would find a likely specimen, a rock laced with a gold color mineral, possibly fool's gold. "*I found one*" would be the cry and the other two would run to look. We would carry the rocks home, carefully tucked into our pockets, only to have Papa declare, "that is sure a pretty stone, I don't believe its gold, but it will look right nice in Mama's flower garden." Mama's flower garden was outlined with many glistening stones, our treasures, collected from Ottery Creek. Drursy, Quartz, Mozarkite, (I later learned this was our state rock) and prurite, malachite and quartz crystal, could be located in Mama's flower beds.

Our farm house was a two story, white frame house, built by my Great-Grandfather back in 1858, just before the Civil War ravaged our part of the country, turning brother against brother, father against son. Our family had felt the results of this hostility and there was still some resentment carried down by cousins on Papa's side of the family. They would speak to each other now, some 60 odd years later, but the family ties had been severed in the war that divided the country.

Papa's Grandfather had fought for the Union. He and other old soldiers would set around the fireplace on winter nights, telling tales of battles, the tales becoming larger with each passing year. One story I can remember was about a mail carrier, shot as he was riding his horse across the West Fork of the Black river. The wisdom of those telling the story was that he was killed by Bushwhackers. Many tales of Bushwhackers still circulated, with families still being accused of having a Bushwhacker in their family tree. According to his tales, Great-Grandfather had fought many battles. As an adult, my research into our family history has shown that this mighty warrior might have exaggerated his heroics. The records show he had served less than three months in the War Between the States. The Court House in Ironton Missouri still bears scars of a battle and I'm sure for many who lived through the war it was a horrific time.

Our barn stood to the left of the house and behind the house about 100 yards, and on the right was our garden spot and an old fruit orchard, planted many years ago. New plum trees sprung up from the fruit that fell to the ground and spoiled, before they could be harvested. There were also a few peach trees and apple trees. Great-Grandfather had built an *apple keeping house* to store our apples in. This consisted of a double walled log structure with a space between the two log walls. This space was filled with saw dust for insulation. There our apples from the orchard kept all winter. Each fall we would take the wagon to the saw mill, operated by Cousin

Latham, and bring back saw dust to fill the space between the logs as the saw dust tended to settle and needed to be replaced.

A corn crib sat behind the garden, close to the corn patch. There was another corn patch on the south side of the house. We raised our own popcorn. On cold winter nights, Mama would pop corn and we would set around the radio, listening to *The Grand Ole Opry*. Once in a-while we would get to listen to *Amos and Andy*. Of course we had to save our batteries and did not listen every night. Electricity did not come into the valley until I finished high school. Some years later, when the next World War began, Mama, Sister, my Grandparents and I would huddle around the radio, listening to President Roosevelt address the citizens of our country with news of the war.

Grandfather had built the corn crib many years ago. It was kept in good repair. Small gage wire lined the walls, so no mice could not get in and eat the corn. Every fall before we filled the corn crib, we checked for cracks in the logs in the walls and the floor. We always grew a lot of corn. We needed corn for the livestock and chickens. We made their feed out of the corn, cracking what we did not use for ourselves, for the livestock. Mama would also can corn and grind the dried corn and make corn meal. It was a staple for our entire homestead. I can still smell the cornbread baking in the oven of the wood stove and see Mama standing at the old wood cook stove, stirring the beans, cooking them in a black, cast iron pot.

We didn't grow our own wheat, so we would buy our flour from the local flour mill, located about two miles down the road, on Ottery Creek. The water from the creek was used to turn the water wheel, which drove the mill and ground the grain. The old mill is gone now, burned to the ground in the 1950's. The Dillard Mill, located close to Cherryville, Missouri looks very similar to our old mill on Ottery Creek.

Mama would make peach cobbler, after the fruit ripened in the orchard, and she canned mason jars full of the golden fruit for a special treat in the winter. Papa would send Brother or me to the cellar on cold winter evenings to bring up a jar of peaches or tomatoes. He loved to have a bowl of peaches or tomatoes with cream poured over them for a treat. I never developed a taste for cream poured my tomatoes, but I still love fresh cream poured over my peaches. The fruit cellar, which is what we called the cellar where we stored all the fruit and vegetables that Mama and Grandmother canned, was located a few feet from the back porch. Rows of jars filled with green beans, corn, tomatoes, pickled okra, spinach, greens, blackberries, pickles, relishes, beets and other vegetables would line the shelves of the cellar, ready for the winter to come. We also stored our rutabagas and potato's and turnips there. Grandfather said the cellar had been there as long as he could recall. I suppose it had been serving as our family's store for several generations.

Working on the Plow

We owned two cows and a calf, Papa's old horse Dolly and a little mule we called Prince, along with pigs that roamed the countryside. Apparently the name Prince went to that little mule's head. When Papa or Grandfather would get the plow ready for planting and plowing the next day, Prince would peek around the barn door, arching his ears in surprise if he saw Papa working on the plow. With ears pinned back, off he would gallop down the lane, toward the mountain on the far side of the valley. A cloud of dust from Princes heels was all that could be seen, as he raced for more pleasant pastures. Over the mountain, digging in his heels, he would lope.

Prince had come to us from Aunt and Uncle's farm. Prince was just a little fellow when he came to our farm. His memories of Uncle's farm was of a place where a young long ear could run and play all day and be a long ear of leisure. Prince was so opposed to work he would gallop forty miles to avoid it. But now he was to take his place on the farm pulling the plow and Prince believed he should still be a long ear of leisure.

Prince Races Over the Mountain

Prince spied Papa working on the plow one spring morning. He turned on his heels and off he raced across the mountain to Uncle's farm never looking back. *"You'll* need to bring Prince back come morning, as it is a far piece to the Latham farm and there isn't enough daylight left for the trip today," Papa sighed. Brother said, "Just wait until I get my hands on that mule." "No" Papa said! "Prince just thinks he was born to royalty and shouldn't have to work. He is a stubborn little cuss. He will grow up and know we all must do our share."

Papa had to set in the shade more often as the plow and the rocky hillside farm had taken its toll. Mama, little Sister, Brother and I helped as much as we could. But we sure needed that ornery little mule. We all knew we had to have good crops come summer time if we were to have enough to eat that winter.

Mama called Brother and me to breakfast before dawn the next morning. "Boys, you need to eat a good breakfast and head over the mountain to bring Prince home. We really need to get the crops in." Brother and I hurried and ate our breakfast, just as the sun woke up that long ago cool spring morning. We were anxious to start our day's journey to Aunt and Uncle's farm. Mama carefully wrapped biscuits in small pieces of cloth and tucked a biscuit into the pocket of each of our bib overalls.

There were panthers, as we called the big mountain lions that shared the mountains with bobcat and other wild critters, who roamed the mountains after sunset. We needed to hurry on our journey to return before night fell and the cats came out. The screams of the panthers could be heard echoing across the hills and valleys through the night, almost like the sound of a woman in great distress. We did not want to meet the huge cats who made those terrible cries.

Papa was still asleep as we started our journey. This gentle man, who had worked so hard to take care of his family, now had to rely on his "*men*" as he called brother and me. At ten and twelve it was sometimes hard to be the men of the family. Papa often told of how he and Mama had married late and had hoped for a family soon. My brother was five years coming, followed by myself and sister. Perhaps the wait had made us more precious to Papa. No harsh words for his children or Mama ever passed his lips. He taught us how to live our lives with the stories he would tell and by his example.

Mama pressed her finger against her lips as we passed Papa sleeping in the front bedroom. She tried to let Papa get as much rest as possible these days. A heaviness in our hearts traveled with us for a short way, our thoughts with Papa, until the noises and beauty of the forest distracted us. Rough cliffs of rhyolite, created from a lava flow millions of years ago, hampered quick travel. Climbing gave way to skinned knees and sore hands. We finally reached the top of the mountain. People from the big mountains back East, would call our St. Francois Mountains, *hills*, but the people in the Ozarks felt these ancient uprisings still deserved the title of mountains, having weathered millions of years.

In earlier days when Papa, Mama, Brother, Sister and I walked across the mountain to Uncle's farm. Papa would tell how the mountain was formed. Molten rock had been pushed up from deep in the earth. The rock formation was called Devil's Honeycomb. Papa would point out the different wild flowers in bloom. Sometimes we gathered the plants for food and medicine. Sassafras, mullein and other plants would be used. Mama liked witch hazel and I needed to tell her we just saw a witch hazel bush. She used it as an astringent at night for her face. She also used it for cuts and bruises. Sometimes we would gargle the witch hazel made into a tea, for sore throats. Mama could come back later in the spring to harvest what she needed.

We passed through a glade, blooming with early wild flowers. Harbinger of spring, a beautiful early spring flower, created a carpet that looked like snow. As the sun rose in the sky, we came to an outcropping of rock which provided a sitting place. Brother declared it was time to eat. He was the oldest by two years and he made the decisions including when I was hungry and when I should eat. We retrieved the biscuits Mama had tucked into our bibs. A small dot of jelly much like a jewel, adored the center of our biscuits. We felt much like princes ourselves. To have jelly at the beginning of spring when the jelly was mainly gone was quiet a treat. Had our mission not lay before us and the sun was climbing higher in the sky, we might have been knights in King Arthur's Court, our swords fashioned from branches lying on the forest floor. But that little old contrary mule needed to be returned to his rightful place plowing the garden. We needed to eat this coming winter. "Let's go little Brother," said Brother, as he saw I had finished my biscuit. I folded my cloth and put it back into my pocket and off we started on our trip again.

Uncle Greets Brother and Me

After a short journey we saw Uncle's farm lying in the valley. We knew an early supper would be laid out for us as Aunt would expect us. We always came after Prince and she would never let us go home hungry. "Just wouldn't be *fittin*," she would say.

We were running across the meadow when terrible sounds met our ears. "*Hee hawing*" and braying and hooves banging on wood, sounds like we had never heard before greeted us. Just then Uncle came out of the barn, a tall stone building made of rocks collected along Ottery Creek. Uncle spied us and smiled, "come and look boys." We hurried to the barn door, sure of Prince's eminent demise. An irate Prince was what we saw, ears laid back and hooves flying. Prince had always had the run of the place when he came to visit before. Green meadows full of tasty timothy and orchard grass were his to munch on all day. Now he was locked in a stall. "That little mule always comes over the mountain when there is work to be done at your place. He thinks he is coming to Aunt and Uncle's for a vacation. I think I have a cure for Princes running away, if you boys agree. You can hitch up old Jack there and take him over to your place to get your crops planted. I'll keep little Prince right here and on this trip he will have a working vacation, much like them boys that come down here from the city, anxious to try their hand at farm work. I don't think your Papa will mind. You boys head on into the house, as Aunt has supper fixed for you two to eat before you start home. I'll put the bridle on Jack, and then I'll join you."

Brother and I ran past the farm bell that would ring the farm hands in from the hayfields for lunch later in the summer. On that cool early spring day, the old cook stove lent a warmth to the kitchen that welcomed us in. "Well, just look at the two of you," Aunt said. "When I saw that little long eared rascal coming across the field yesterday, I told Uncle, our boys will be here tomorrow and I must fry some chicken and make them a rhubarb pie. Now you boys get over to that pump and get those hands clean." Brother worked the pump while I washed up, then I returned the favor.

We took our places at Aunt's table, folding our hands as Uncle offered grace. "Lord, little Prince needs to learn where his home is and what his role in life will be. Let him understand the lessons I have for him. Lord, bless these boys' Mama and Papa and sister. Take our boys safely across the mountain on their journey home with Jack. Amen Lord." We all said *amen*, ready to tackle some chicken and then pie. That pie was setting on top of the stove's warming oven and seemed to be calling to me.

After eating our fill, it was time to head back over the mountain with Jack, Uncle's old mule. Aunt leaned down and placed the usual kisses on top of our heads. Aunt was a tall, rawboned looking mountain woman. Her white hair was piled high on her head and an apron always covered her print dress and her glasses were perched low on her nose. A flat, brown mole graced her left cheek. Her blue eyes twinkled when she smiled, and she smiled often.

Aunt had worked hard, as the story goes, farmed out to a hotel in Ironton after her Mama died. She washed clothes on a board, standing for long hours each day, from the time she was twelve until she was sixteen and met Uncle. They married, moved to this farm and raised eight children. The children were all gone, moved off to find work in St. Louis. Aunt said empty arms needed filling and when we came to call, we fit perfectly. But for now, let's go back to this story. We will leave Aunt's story for a later telling.

Uncle had a bridle on Jack, Uncle's mule, and he seemed to know what to do. He fell in behind us, Brother barely holding the reins. Prince looked our way, but in his princely way tossed his head and said with a hee haw, "I'm still on vacation." "Oh is this little royal one in for a surprise. In the morning we have a field to plow. I'll bring him home in a few of weeks and he will not dream of his vacation spot again," Uncle smiled and winked.

Across the mountain with Jack we went. "Do you think Prince will stay home when Uncle returns him," I asked Brother? "I don't know but I bet Papa will get a laugh about Princes working vacation," Brother replied. That night we told Mama and Papa about Princes plight. "Oh, Uncle will take very good care of Prince, but his vacation days have ended," Papa said.

Jack Works Hard, Plowing the Garden

Jack worked hard tilling the garden, pulling timber from the woods and other farm work. Grandfather would fall a tree, then cut it up with a cross cut saw. Brother would man the other end of the saw. My job was to load the wood onto the sled. Then Jack would pull the sled home and Brother and I would unload the wood, ready for the winter cold that was to come.

Jack seemed quite content with himself, having learned the ways of being a mule early. He would let us know when he needed to rest or have a drink, by slowing down. Uncle had told us, "boys, mules know what they need, and if you listen to them, they will let you know what it is they want. If you pay attention, you will never have a stubborn mule. They respond very well to having their needs met and some kindness shown to them, much like humans. Jack will work hard all day, with the correct care." Jack knew just what to do and we had our garden planted in record time. Every morning Brother and I would look at the garden, observing the growth of our plants. The afternoon sun warmed the seeds and they sprouted, despite the cold spring mornings.

Soon we were harvesting the pea crop, and lettuce was on the table every night. Nothing was better than the sweet taste of the spring peas, along with new potatoes. The corn was beginning to grow down in the corn patch and tassels were forming too. Green beans were ready for picking and Grandmother, Sister and Mama spent many hot afternoons sitting on the porch, snapping beans, peeling peaches and other garden vegetables. Papa sometimes would join them, no longer able to help in the garden, but if it was not too hot, he would help snap the beans or peel the fruit. The cellar was beginning to be filled to overflowing with jars of garden produce.

The smell of garlic and dill would drift from the kitchen, as Mama made pickles for winter. I forgot to mention, Mama had an herb garden just behind the kitchen. She grew dill, garlic, sage, and feverfew, which she used for headaches, and fennel for sweet pickles. She grew Rosemary, and when the weather was warm, our dog would get a bath, with Rosemary mixed into his bath water. Mama said this dispelled fleas. Of course we would find Golden Seal growing in the woods and Mama would make a tea of the Golden Seal for our colds and we chewed on the root for fever blisters. Most of our doctoring came from Mama's herb garden and the forest surrounding our homestead.

June fifteenth had arrived. This was the day we sat aside to plant our pumpkins and winter squash. When fall arrived, we would sell pumpkins at the store at Black, Missouri. A buyer from St Louis would come with a truck and take the pumpkins back to the farmers markets in the city. We planted the pumpkins and squash where the spinach and peas, our early crops had been. We wasted no garden space. The small amounts of money we earned from our harvest supplied the things we needed that we could not grow on the farm. We anticipated the delight of a red tomato about July 4th. The first ripe tomatoes of the year were and still are an indescribable treat.

The wood pile was full, thanks to Jack and his hard work, pulling the sled filled with wood from the forest. Papa was always very concerned about what we now call conservation, making sure not to harvest young trees. He taught us how to harvest to save the forest. *Clear Cutting* was a very bad word in Papa's vocabulary. Many days were spent in years past, helping Papa cut and load the wood, but this year Brother and I had the job all to ourselves. Papa was very sad when he could not assist us. "I'm sorry boys, but I just can't go to the woods today. I wish I could be of more help." Papa always looked wistful when he said this. He had worked so hard to take care of the three of us and Mama, but now he could no longer work. He looked out at the wood shed and declared, "Boys, you have done a very good job."

A few weeks later we spied Uncle coming up the lane with Prince trotting behind. Brother and I ran to meet Uncle and Prince. Prince snorted a hello and nuzzled first Brother, then me as we hugged his neck. "Well boys, I believe Prince will stay home from now on. He certainly had a lot of work to do this visit. He was no longer a long ear of leisure on this trip over the mountain," Uncle rubbed Prince's ear as he spoke.

Mama heard Uncle's voice and came out of the kitchen, onto the porch. "Now Bill," Bill was Uncle's first name, although we just called him Uncle, "you're not going to get away from here without some dinner." Uncle stammered and then said, "Why of course I will stay for dinner Sis." Mama hurried and set another plate as she was sure Uncle would need to walk Jack home across the mountain before dark sat in.

Mama wanted to hear all about Uncle's family and how the kids, as Mama called Uncles children, although they were all in their forties, were doing in St Louis. "Well", said Uncle, "Young Bill is still working on the streetcar. He has the line all the way from Broadway to the Mississippi River." "It sounds as if young Bill is doing quite well for himself," Mama reckoned. Uncle replied, "Well at least he has a job, and many people don't these days. He seems to like his new job. Someday Maude and I will go to St Louis and ride on his street car." (Maude was Aunt's given name.) "Sally," (Aunt and Uncle's youngest daughter), "has three Grandchildren now. Can you believe I'm a Great-Grand Pa?" With that Uncle gave a chuckle. "I expect they will be down for Thanksgiving. Maybe they'll come for the sorghum making." My ears perked up at the mention of sorghum making. Sorghum making was one of my favorite times in the entire year. I had just looked at the lower patch of the garden. It seemed as if it were growing taller each day. Dinner was finished and Brother hurried out to the barn to put the halter on Jack, although I believe he would have followed Uncle without a halter. Jack cut quite a shine, when he saw Uncle, bellowing a few brays of welcome, to greet Uncle. Uncle bid us all goodbye, giving Mama and Sister a kiss on the cheek, and a handshake to Papa, Brother and me. He then headed down the lane to cross Bell Mountain to his home on the other side.

Prince never ran away again, but for learning his role of a well- disciplined mule, I'm not sure. Let me tell you of some of Prince's escapades during his learning. Prince's first job was to plow the ground to break up the soil and ready the ground for Brother and me to plant the seeds in the garden.

Papa brought out the plow early one morning. As usual Prince looked around the barn and at the dirt road that had been his escape route. Brother and I watched Prince as he considered his options. Maybe he was thinking of all his hard work at Uncle's farm? Then he spied Papa's straw hat. That hat had a golden glow in the early morning sun. As Papa bent over the plow, Prince sauntered over to Papa and snatched his hat. Away went Prince and away went Papa's gold hat. "Boys," cried Papa, "get my hat back and catch that mule." Papa was not feeling well and was in no mood to play games with Prince. Brother and I chased Prince around the barnyard. "You go the other way and I will chase Prince around to you," Brother shouted, running as fast as he could. Prince was looking back at Brother when I caught him. Prince and the hat were returned to Papa and Prince was hitched to the plow.

Prince worked hard until lunch time, when we all stopped for lunch. Papa led Prince to barnyard and shut the gate. "Boys, get Prince some grain and water. I don't want to turn him loose in the meadow until we finish the plowing." After lunch Papa again hitched Prince to the plow. Papa kept a tight hold on his hat whenever he was close to Prince. Prince had found a new game. Maybe running away was no longer fun but this new game appeared to have some appeal for Prince.

That night after supper, Papa suggested we all go down to Ottery Creek and cool off. "Can Prince and Tip come too," I asked? "I suppose so," Papa replied, "Just make sure he leaves my hat alone." Mama had made Brother and I swim suits from material from Papa's old shirts. This was the first year we had official *bathing suits*. Our suits looked just like the ones we saw in the Sears & Roebuck Catalog. Mama had made Sister a pretty suit. I remember it had blue flowers on it, made from a feed sack. Sister had pretty blue eyes and red curly hair and she looked like Shirley Temple, a child movie star. Brother, Sister and I had never been to a movie, but we had a radio and we had heard about Shirley Temple and I was sure Sister looked just like her.

We ran down the path leading to Ottery Creek and to our favorite swimming hole. Tip, our dog, was in the water first, followed by Brother and me. Little Sister hung back just a bit, not wanting to mess up her new bathing suit. Prince stood on the water's edge, leaning his neck down to get a drink. Tip raced circles around Prince, barking as he ran. Prince had tolerated this dog play as long as he could. He began nipping and whinnying at Tip and soon Tip became tired of his play. Prince lay down and rolled in the shallow water, and Tip followed in imitation.

Mama and Papa sat on the bank of the creek and put their feet in the water. Mama looked for pretty stones close to where she was sitting. We could hear her tell Papa from time to time, "Oh look, here's another pretty one. At last Papa said it was time to return home. We voiced our usual protest about not long enough; while we began drying off on a towel Mama had brought along. The night was beginning to drift over Bell Mountain and close in on our valley. Now and then one of us would swat a mosquito as it buzzed our heads as we walked the path back to our house. Mama said as she climbed the porch steps, "Papa, you and Sister sit here on the porch and I will bring some cookies I made this morning before the heat of the day sat in. Boys, go down to the spring house and bring us up that crock of buttermilk. But don't go wasting time catching frogs in the spring branch. Copperheads like the spring branch and frogs too," Mama said as she went into the kitchen to bring out a platter of cookies. Brother and I returned as fast as we could, not wanting to encounter a copperhead on our path, or let Sister eat more than her share of the cookies!

We sat on the porch and Mama said, "listen to the spring peepers, they've been singing since early spring. Looks like their voices would be tired by now. Oh, do you hear those bass voices of the bull frogs? I think we will call this our Ottery Creek Opera". The porch swing creaked as Mama gently swayed to the music. "Can't you just see the conductor waving his wand," she asked? The music would rise and fall, as if under the direction of an unseen conductor, his wand held high, bringing the music to a crescendo, a slight pause, then the conductor would wave his wand and the music would start again.

We sat on the porch and listened to the Opry provided by the critters that lived in the spring fed pound. A soft breeze brought the aroma of honeysuckle drifting over the porch. Mama wrapped her arms around herself as she said, "Papa, don't you feel and smell the fall in the air? The days may be hot, but fall is coming. Children, that means school time is almost here. I do declare you boys have both out grown your pants. Look at you, your pants almost to your knees. Grandmother and Grandfather are coming for a few days. Grandmother will help me make some new overalls for you boys and Sister some new dresses. Papa, can you believe this is our little girls first year of school?"

Papa said, "No Mama, I can't believe she is almost a grown up lady. School time means harvest time. I was looking at the corn this afternoon. I believe we will need to pick some of it before long, as it getting dry. Boys, you will need to help me drag that corn sheller out of the barn tomorrow morning. I need to make sure it is oiled up and ready to go. Mama do you remember when we had to shell all that corn by hand? Now all I have to do is hitch Prince up to the corn- sheller and put the corn in. Why, Sister could do that job all by herself. It was hard to get the money for that piece of machinery but it will sure save lots of hard work."

"Papa, when will it be sorghum making time," I asked? That was my favorite time in the fall. All the neighbors got together at the Mont Black's farm down the road. We would all haul our cane in on wagons. Uncle and Aunt would be there along with lots of valley children to play with. There were five children in the Black Family and the Bells and the Shy families would be there also. Most all of the children we went to school with would be there. Uncle's mule, Jack would be the lead mule, making the sorghum mill go round and round, and then Prince would take over, or at least that was the plan. Maybe there would not be too many hats to steal or other mischief for Prince to get into. "Well now," Papa said, "the cane won't be ready until after school starts in September. When the weather is cool, it will be molasses making time."

The coming of fall meant we would be wearing shoes most of the time. During the summer months Brother, Sister and I would wear shoes only when we got to church, much like the other children of Ottery. Shoe leather was costly. Mama would carry a bag with a wet wash cloth. Sister would wash her feet first, then she would put on her socks and shoes, then Brother and I would have a turn. Little Sister did not want to put her shoes on at the church steps. "Mama," she would say, "I don't want my friends seeing me put my shoes on at the church door. Can't I put my shoes on before I get to church?" We found a log not too far from the church and put our shoes on there. Sister didn't know most of the other children did the same thing. Saving our shoes for winter was a necessity for all the children.

On this particular Sunday, Sister was spared the embarrassment of having to wash her feet and put her shoes on. We were to ride to church. Brother pulled the wagon into the church yard on that Sunday morning, still warm with the end of summer heat. A small crowd had gathered at the steps leading into the church. "Well, I wonder who that man in the straw hat and suit is, standing next to the Preacher," Mama questioned? A small thin man with spectacles was gesturing and seemed quite excited. On the ground lay some cardboard boxes. Preacher Fullbright called to Mama and Papa, "come over and meet Mr. Mirth. I can't divulge too much information. You will have to wait until service is over for my announcement." It seemed Preacher would never finish his sermon that morning. As we rose to sing our last song, Preacher motioned for Mr. Mirth, with the fancy store bought suit, to come to the pulpit. Mr. Mirth raised his hand and Aunt Latham struck a chord on the organ. A beautiful baritone voice came from the little man and we joined to sing, *Sing the Wondrous love of Jesus.* When we came to the chorus, Mr. Mirth shouted, "every one sing!" The voices seemed to raise the roof. *"We will sing and shout the victory."* "Now if you will all be seated," the Preacher said, "I have an exciting announcement. Mr. Mirth has come all the way from New York City, to teach our children and any adults that wish to avail themselves of this opportunity to sing and to learn to read music. Can't you hear the glorious voices of our church as they raise their musically trained voices to praise the Lord? I will allow Mr. Mirth, a teacher and composer, to give you the wonderful news." Preacher shook Mr. Mirth's hand as he spread his other hand to the congregation. Mr. Mirth seemed to rise on his toes as he said, "ladies and gentlemen, we are to have a singing school. It will start the week before school and all you had to do to attend the school is to buy a song book. That book cost one dollar. In the book there is a song called **Peace,** that I composed and it is published in the song book. I will gladly spend one night and take meals with each of your families. This will allow me to spend more time with your young people and give you extra lessons. The regular lessons will be held at the school. I will be at the back of the church with your Preacher and will be glad to talk to each of you about the school. I hope you will avail your children and perhaps yourself, of this wonderful opportunity."

Sister fairly danced out of the church, she was so excited. Sister wanted so much to attend the singing school. She fancied herself a singer like Lily Mae Ledford of *the Coon Creek Girls*. She had heard Lily Mae and Black-eyed Susie sing *Little Birdie* and for weeks all we heard was Little Birdie, Little Birdie. Actually little Sister's singing was quite good. I certainly did not want to tell her how well she could sing. Brothers were not supposed to tell little sisters things like that.

I could see Papa secretly counting the cost of the school. Three dollars! That was an awful lot of money. "Papa," Mama said, "I believe we have extra eggs to sell as the chickens have been laying quite well for the past few weeks. Maybe we could go to the store at Black and sell them tomorrow." The school was to start next week. Sister was listening to every word Papa spoke. "Mama, I believe we could just about manage the cost of the school." Sister began clapping her hands and was so excited she could hardly shake Mr. Mirth's hand.

Papa asked Mr. Mirth to honor us with his company on Sunday night after church and spend at least Monday and maybe Tuesday in our home. "My wife makes real good fried chicken, and the best blackberry cobbler and bread pudding in the county," Papa said as he shook hands with Mr. Mirth. Mr. Mirth smiled and shook Papa's hand, "I would deem it a privilege to spend some time in your home Sir." Mr. Mirth was smiling as he said this. I believe he was thinking of fried chicken and blackberry cobbler.

Mr. Scott, was noted for his bass singing, which could make a church pew vibrate, said as he shook Mr. Mirth's hand, "I will be attending your school. I believe this music is also called Sacred Harp music, am I not correct?" "Yes you are correct Mr. "Uh"-- Scott," stated Mr. Mirth. Mr. Scott was a bit put out that Mr. Mirth did not immediately remember his name. After all, he was the most important part of the church's music, after the pianist. Mr. Mirth, sensing Mr. Scott's displeasure, grasped his hand and unruffled Mr. Scott's feathers saying,has "Mr. Scott, I heard you singing in church and your voice will be a definite asset to our school. I shall be very pleased if you were to come to our school." The air seemed to leave Mr. Scott's chest and he said, "Sir, you may count on my presence at your singing school."

Mr. Mirth came home with us in the wagon after he had shook hands with all the people at church and had obtained the names of students who wished to attend his school. I could see Prince eye Mr. Mirth up and down and Prince took special note of his hat. I must keep an eye on Prince while Mr. Mirth was around; for I am sure he would not take too kindly to having his hat snatched by that ornery little mule. Brother snapped the reins and Prince trotted down the dirt road with Mr. Mirth and Papa on the front seat of the wagon and Mama, Sister and me in the back.

When we arrived home, Mama went into the kitchen and Papa, Brother, Mr. Mirth and I sat down in the parlor. "Well," said Papa,

"Tell me where your home is Mr. Mirth." I could tell Mr. Mirth was from somewhere far away, as he talked different from the people around these parts. "I was raised in up- state New York in the foot hills of the Adirondack Mountains, in a little town called Lyons Fall. It sat on a creek called the Black Creek. I was wondering if your Black River would look like the Black Creek and the Black River where I lived, but it sure doesn't. Your waters are clear and sparkling. The water of Black River and Black Creek in New York has a black color. It seems the water falls over, in places, a natural tannic acid, causing the water to appear black. I was surprised to see your Black River is clear. Where does the name Black River come from? I noticed Ottery Creek is very clear also," Mr. Mirth noted. Papa said, "I'm not sure where the name Black River or for that matter Ottery Creek came from. I guess I always thought the Black name may have come from a family named Black that had settled here, but I'm not sure. A man named Munger, from New York like your-self, settled here in the early years and he was a fur trapper. Perhaps he trapped otter and that is where Ottery Creek obtained its name. Boys, that would be a good subject for your history class at school. You ask your teacher when school starts if he knows where our names for these places came from. But, back to you Mr. Mirth, tell us more about yourself."

Mama came into the parlor and announced lunch was ready. Sister had helped set the table and was very proud of the fact that she had placed the silverware in exactly the right places. Papa praised her, saying "Why Grace, you have done a fine job of helping Mama set the table. Mr. Mirth will think he is back in New York, dining in one of those fancy New York restaurants."

Mr. Mirth survived the food on the table and exclaimed, "I'm sure this fine meal could equal all the fancy foods in New York." Mama blushed and asked Mr. Mirth, to take a seat at the opposite end of the table from Papa. "Mr. Mirth, will you please ask the blessing," Papa requested. We held hands and Mr. Mirth asked the blessing for our good food.

"We have yet to hear about your life Mr. Mirth. Tell us how you came to be a music teacher," asked Papa, who was always interested in others and how they came to be who they were.

"I was raised outside a town of about 500 people. We had an old piano that belonged to my Grandmother. My parents found out early that I could set down at that piano and pick out some songs. There was an older lady in town, Mrs. Jeargin. She was the wife of the town doctor. She had been trained at a music conservatory in New York City. Her parents sent her there when she was young. She had married the town Doctor after she returned home from school, and she never left the area again. Her son was grown by the time I was a youngster, and her husband had died. She began to give music lessons in her home, and somehow my parents came up with the quarter a week to provide me voice and piano lessons." I took lessons until I was an older teenager. I then joined the Army, desiring to become a member of the Army Band."

"Then the Great War began and I went to France, then on to Germany, marching all the way, but not to band music. There was not much time to play or study music, tromping through the rain, snow and mud. My feet froze and I lost one toe. That is why I walk with a slight limp. But I fared much better than many of the poor boys, who never returned home. When my ship sailed into the New York Harbor and I saw the Statue of Liberty, I must say I shed my fair share of tears at that sight. In addition to the war, influenza, which was called Spanish Flu, was raging across Europe and America. Our ship was quarantined in the harbor for over a month, because of an outbreak aboard ship. I didn't get as sick as many did. Several of my buddies survived the war, but didn't get home, dying of the flu on the ship and several more passed away on trains, bound for their loved ones and home. I was one of the lucky ones."

"That flu made it to these parts of the country too," Papa replied. "I had two aunts and a cousin die from the Spanish Flu. It sure was deadly. At times there were so many sick people, it was hard to find pall-bearers for the deceased. You sure were one of the lucky ones. We all felt that way too. Mama and I were both just young *whipper-snappers* then, weren't we Mama?" "Now Mr. Mirth, please continue on with your story, and Papa, stop your foolishness" Mama teased.

"Well, after I returned from the war, I began to play for dances held in homes, then in dance halls. Rag time was all the rage at that time, and I mastered many rags. My favorite piece by was composed by Scott Joplin, a master of Rag Time. It was called Bink's Waltz. He composed this piece for his small son, who had passed away. Then the depression came and people did not have the money to pay me to provide music for their festivities. I had been composing music and sold one of my songs to the *Hartman Music Company* in western Missouri. As part of the promotion of my music, I am traveling the country, teaching music at singing schools, like the one we will have here. I will continue to compose songs and hopefully sell some of them. One of my greatest joys is seeing people enjoy my music, as it is all written to praise the Lord, I hope people also receive a blessing from the songs I write," Mr. Mirth concluded.

Supper was finished and Papa suggested we adjourn to the parlor. "Mr. Mirth, we have an old pump organ. Would you favor us with some music," Papa asked as he led the way to the parlor? With great flourish, Mr. Mirth took his seat at the organ. He gave the pedals a few pumps, and then began playing and singing *Barbara Allen*. Of course we all joined in as we had been singing that song for as long as I could remember. Mr. Mirth smiled and said, "I thought you folks might know *Barbara Allen*. Tell me how you began singing that song, if you wouldn't mind." Papa answered, "I never really thought about where the song came from. My Grandmother sang that song when I was just a little boy. She told me she had learned it from her Grandmother." "Well," said Mr. Mirth, "my research tells me that song came over with the very early settlers from England and Scotland. It seems the song may have originated in Scotland. The thought is that it may have been composed in the 1500's. The earliest written record of that song was from the 1600's. I would imagine your ancestors, along with other Scottish and English immigrants brought that song over from Scotland. It made its way across the Appalachian Mountains into the Ozarks by descendants of those early settlers."

"I'm not only teaching music in the Singing Schools as I travel, but I am also collecting as many of the folk songs as I can. The harmony is so unusual. I love the high harmony that seems to come so naturally to the folks here and other places in the South. Would you mind singing more of the songs your Grandmother taught you?" Mr. Mirth was anxious to learn some of our musical history.

It seemed Papa was tired by this time, but he said, "Mama would you sing my favorite song?" Mama said, "Well if Mr. Mirth would like to hear it, I would be glad to sing it for you Papa." Mama began to sing, "*There shall I visit the place of my birth. There shall I gaze on the mountains again.* She finished and Mr. Mirth said, "That is one of the most beautiful ballads I have ever heard. Would you sing it again, please? I would like to write the words down and also write the music. I have never heard that song before. Where did you hear that song?" Mama replied, "Just like the other song, we just always sang it." I can remember my Mama singing that song while she worked in the kitchen. Cooking and cleaning always seemed to give way to a song. She sang a lot of other songs too. I bet you could have her sing some of them for you. I believe they will be joining us for supper tomorrow night. I would imagine her and Papa will be at the singing school tomorrow. But if not, you can see her tomorrow night.

Mama said, "We'll get a tablet and pencil for you if you would like." Mama asked me to fetch a tablet from the desk in her bedroom.

"Papa, are you too tired for anymore music tonight," Mama questioned Papa? Papa was beginning to look tired after a long day. Mr. Mirth looked at Papa and said, "Maybe we should postpone more music until tomorrow." Mama allowed this would be a good idea and helped Papa to their bedroom. "Boys, will you show Mr. Mirth where he will sleep, and see if he needs anything, "Mama requested.

Brother and I showed Mr. Mirth to his room at the top of the stairs. Sister had already retired. Mama had carried her up to her room shortly after the music began. It seemed the excitement had overwhelmed her and her eyes could not stay open. Mr. Mirth spent the night sleeping in the room I shared with Brother, while we got to sleep in the barn.

How exciting it was for us to sleep in the hay loft. "Now, be sure and put out the lantern safely, as we don't want the barn to burn down boys," Papa called from the dark of his and Mama's bedroom. Mama gave us kisses and told us to keep warm. The night was still heavy with the heat of the day as Brother and I carried our blankets and lantern to the barn. Brother and I were not allowed to sleep in the barn often, only when there was company and Mama was sure it was not too cold for us. We spread a blanket over the fresh hay, and then we snuggled under another blanket. The cows seemed to be a bit surprised at their new bed partners, but after a bit of mooing, maybe it was time for feeding they may have thought, they settled down and went on chewing their cud, safe in their stalls.

Dawn came quickly and Fred, the rooster flapped his wings, threw his head back and let go with a tremendous *cock a doodle do*. His crow in the barn was much louder than when it was heard from the distance of our upstairs bedroom. Fred sounded like a bugler sounding the morning alarm in a barracks. Brother would know that sound in a few years. We didn't know at the time, but WWII was just around the corner and Brother would be off to Europe, far from our little home in the Ozarks. Many of the other boys would leave too.

All of Mont Black's boys would go to war, along with the Wells, the Lathams and the Hayfields and others. Some would not return. The Hayfields have a boy buried in the fields of Flanders. They often talked of a trip to see their boy's grave, but there never seemed to be enough money or time for them to make that trip.

But all was well with our world now, as we ran for the house, Mama, Papa and little Sister, and breakfast. We hurried for the table, but Mama stopped us, "Not so fast, boys. You two go wash up. You boys know the rules. Comb your hair as you both look like you slept in the hay," she laughed. "We do have company and I want my young men to look like gentlemen."

Mr. Mirth came down the stairs, looking dapper in his suit and bow tie. "Good morning ladies and gentlemen. It looks like a fine morning. Are you young people ready for school today?"

Sister could hardly set still. "Oh yes," she exclaimed, clapping her hands together! I think she had visions of herself on stage at a famous opera house. Of course we did not know quite what that would look like. Maybe she would be on the *Grand Ole Opry*, like the *Coon Creek girls*, or one of the girls in the *Carter Family*. Papa asked Mr. Mirth to say grace over our breakfast. I hoped Mr. Mirth would not pray for very long as I was really hungry. Mr. Mirth prayed a short prayer and breakfast was finished without a much more conversation; Sister could not have stood a delay in her destiny.

Papa told Brother to hitch up Prince after breakfast and he could drive Mr. Mirth, Sister and me to school. Mama carefully counted out three dollars from the cookie jar and gave it to Mr. Mirth. "Thank you Madame," he said as he shook hands with Mama. He went into the hallway and took three books from his suitcase. "Children, here are your books for the singing school," he said, handing each of us a book with a harp on the front. Sister carefully took her book, holding it as if holding something very precious. "Oh I can hardly wait," she whispered.

Brother was just leading Prince around to the front to hitch up the wagon when Mr. Mirth, with his straw hat perched on his head and suitcases in both hands, walked outside and down the steps. Mr. Mirth opened the gate and proceeded to the wagon. Prince took one look at that hat and here he came, snatched Mr. Mirth's hat right off his head and off he went! Brother and I, both shouting, chased after him! Around the barn yard we all went. Finally I caught Prince and carefully took Mr. Mirth's hat out of Prince's mouth. He let go of the hat easily, apparently tired of his little game. Mama and Papa were so upset, but Mr. Mirth said he had a little horse when he was a youngster so as not to worry, he knew all about horses and mules and at times, they needed a little entertainment also.

Mr. Mirth asked Mama if she would sing the song she had begun last night, tonight after supper. "I would surely appreciate your singing that song again. I would like to write it down and perhaps set the notes to paper," Mr. Mirth requested. Mama said she would be glad to sing it again, if he truly wanted to put it to paper.

I was not happy as I climbed aboard the wagon, taking my seat behind Brother and Mr. Mirth. Prince's bad behavior had made for a grumpy start to my day. I gave Sister a hand up. Mother told us to be good and Brother gave the reins a snap and down the road Prince trotted. He seemed in high spirits, not a bit ashamed of his bad behavior.

Brother pulled the wagon into the school yard and jumped down to tie Prince to the hitching post. Prince had proved he could not be trusted to wander the school yard munching on grass to his heart's content today. Prince shook his head and snorted, not pleased with his lack of freedom.

Several other wagons pulled into the school yard. Some students were walking down the lane to the school house. Mr. Mirth thanked Brother for the ride, and he climbed down from the wagon. "Let me help you with the boxes Mr. Mirth," I called. I carried one box into the school house. It was heavy with the weight of the books Mr. Mirth hoped to sell.

Mr. Mirth was already in the school room, moving desks to the back of the room. "I want room for us to stand," he said, a little out of breath. "We need to breathe from our diaphragms, so we need to be standing." The room was quickly filling up with budding singers. Mr. Mirth began to divide the room into sections, "ladies on the right, gentlemen on the left," he called. "Next I will ask you each to sing for me. I would like to decide if you are tenor, high tenor, bass, alto or soprano." Sister could barely wait for her turn to find what section she would sing in. First the Davis family each took a turn. Genelle Davis sang a stanza and Mr. Mirth seemed quite pleased as he moved her to the alto section. "If all of you can sing like Miss Davis, we will have quite a choir come next Sunday," Mr. Mirth clasped his hands together, smiling. The rest of the Davis family did not disappoint Mr. Mirth as he placed all seven in different sections. "Mr. Scott, I do not believe you will need to audition as I heard your wonderful bass voice last Sunday." Mr. Mirth motioned for Mr. Scott to take his place to the left of the tenor section. We only had one other bass voice, as many of the young men attending the school had voices that had not yet deepened. Mont Black seemed to be able to sing either bass or tenor and as the bass section needed filling out, Mr. Mirth placed him in the bass section. Finally it was Sister's turn. She took a deep breath and sang the soprano part quite wonderfully. "Why Miss Grace, you did a wonderful job, you will be in the soprano section," Mr. Mirth smiled at Sister. I was not looking forward to my time to sing. Boys of my age did not much care for performing in public, although Brother did not seem to mind quite as much as I did. We both ended up in the high tenor section. I wasn't too happy with my assignment. I would much rather have sang bass, but a ten year old boy doesn't have the range for a bass singer. I imagined a bass voice to be quite manly.

After Mr. Mirth was satisfied with the placements in the choir, he directed our attention to the blackboard. "If you will notice the different shapes I have drawn on the blackboard. Each note is as-signed a particular shape to indicate a certain pitch. Now I will sing the shapes as I point to the, then you will join with me in singing do-re-me-fa-sol-la-ti-do. Now, take a deep breath and breathe from your diaphragm and sing with me," Mr. Mirth directed. Little Sister drew herself up to her full height and sang as loud as she could. She sounded as if she had mastered the sound of each shape. It wasn't long before all of the singers could read the shape of the *notes* in the book. There were some new songs we learned along with some of our old favorites.

Mr. Mirth came home with us after the singing school, to spend his final night with us, in our home. He would move on to the Mont Black home after the school tomorrow. He again reminded Mama of her promise to sing the song about the *Mist Covered Mountains*. After supper that night we all adjourned to the parlor, Papa resting in his chair. He appeared very tired and I knew he would be retiring soon. Mr. Mirth sat at the organ with pad and pen in hand. Mama said, "Mr. Mirth, I believe you asked me about the history of the song I sang last night. I truly don't remember, it was just another of those songs we had always sang." As Mama began to sing, he quickly wrote down the words. He then asked her to sing it again as he accompanied her on the organ, listening carefully to each note sung. After each rendition, he would play the song again and again and then quickly record the notes he had played. I could tell Mama was tiring of singing, after the fourth time of singing the same song. I believe Mr. Mirth sensed her weariness also, as he told her this would be the final time she would need to sing the song.

Mama looked over at Papa. He had dosed off to sleep. She told Mr. Mirth we must take our leave, as morning would come before we knew it. Mr. Mirth told Mama how much he appreciated her sharing and singing her song for him. With that he headed up the stairs, note pad in hand. I'm sure he intended to refine Mama's song, sitting by the table, with the coal oil lamp and the full moon providing his only light. Brother and I headed off to the barn with the usual warning from Papa to extinguish the lantern before we went to sleep.

On the third day of the singing school, Mr. Mirth declared today would be a fun day. We would pit the ladies against the men. Mr. Mirth would decide who won the contest. I could see Sister was all excited about the contest. Actually I was a bit excited myself. I would like to have told Papa that we had beat the girls singing. But I don't think Sister could *have* born that defeat. Try as we might, the men could not beat the ladies singing *I'll Fly Away* and *The Old Gospel Ship*.

I knew Sister would have been hard to live with had she been defeated by her brothers at the singing school. I was secretly thankful the ladies had won.

The school lasted five days, then Mr. Mirth moved on to other schools. We never heard from him again. I often wondered about him and where he had gone. Our only connection to him was the song books we had purchased. Sister still has hers and she still hums a bit of his song that was published in that book from the *Hartman Music Company, now and then*. Did he write more songs? Maybe he traveled back to his home in New York State, living in his old home by the Black River. I would like to think he continued teaching music and started a family after the depression was over. When I think back, I realize how many people, like Mr. Mirth, had to rely on strangers to provide a place to sleep and food to eat during the Depression. The people in our valley welcomed him in and shared their homes and their tables with Mr. Mirth and other travelers who passed through our hills during those times, in search of work and food. I remember Aunt Bessie Goggins telling of a stranger who shared their table and slept in their barn one night. Later they heard Jesse James, an infamous outlaw had robbed a train at Gads Hill the day the stranger came to their home, in search of a place to sleep and food to eat. She believed it was Jesse James. I always wondered if it was Jesse, where did the other members of his gang stay. There were no other reports from neighbors of strangers staying at their homes that night.

Papa kept about six bee hives in the orchard. Grandfather called the bee hives "Bee Gums," as long ago, settlers placed their hives in hollow black gum tree logs. Grandfather said the settlers made do with the materials they found in nature. Hence the fallen trees, with hollowed out logs made excellent bee hives. Grandfather said he remembered his Grand- Pappy keeping bees in the bee gum logs along the rock fences that bordered his fields. Father and Grandfather had smokers and could get honey from the hives without getting stung. They had hats with veils and always wore long sleeves when robbing the hives. Grandfather said the bees could sense if you were "*scared*" and then they would chase you and sting you if they caught you. I tried to stay away from those hives because I was scared of those bees. I sure did like the honey, just wanted someone other than me to take the honey away from the bees.

Although we had our own hives, Grandfather still liked the old way of robbing a bee tree. I suppose it was the "*thrill*" of the hunt that enticed him. Grandfather, Papa and several of the neighbors would pick a late evening to *rob a bee tree*. Grandfather said you needed to go after the heat of the day was gone, so the bees would be calmer. Last year Grandfather said Brother was old enough to go bee tree robbing. Grandfather had located a bee tree while he was coon hunting last fall. Grandfather said, "There is a science to finding a bee tree." If you see some bees along a creek *watering*, you can follow them back to the hive." He marked the bee tree with a hatchet so another bee hive robber would not steal the honey before Grandfather had a chance to rob it himself. It was an Ozark tradition, to mark your bee tree with three chops of the hatchet. Others, looking at the tree would know someone had already found that tree and they would not rob the tree themselves. Grandfather had checked the tree out a few days before the bee robbing expedition was to take place and found the bees still had a hive in that tree. Brother was all excited about being included with the men. I was sure glad I was too young for that adventure. I was dreading the day when I could go with the men, robbing the bee tree for honey. The thoughts of bees, covering my arms was not an experience I wanted to have.

I had seen Papa and Grandfather covered with bees. They wore hats with veils and long sleeved shirts and gloves. Somehow they were never stung. I guess they weren't afraid of the bees and the bees knew they weren't.

Papa was still able to go *bee tree robbing* last year. He was feeling poorly but still wanted to go. Grandfather said they would not need to hurry as the bees would still be there when they arrived. Grandfather felt Papa would be able to go and not get too tired. "That is," he winked, "if the bees don't decide to chase us."

Several neighbors had gathered at our house one evening. Grandmother, Mrs. Black and Mama and some other neighbors would visit while the men went bee tree robbing. The fellows were all equipped with buckets to collect the honey from the bee hive. Papa called to Mama, "bring out some old rags please." They would smoke out the bees with the rags and coal oil. The cool evening air and the smoke would calm the bees and prevent a swarm from stinging the robbers. Papa, Grandfather and Brother and several neighbors set out, coal-oil, bucket and rags in hand, to smoke out the bees. Off the men went, leaving me, little sister and Mama and Grandmother and some of the neighbor ladies behind to visit. This was one time I was glad to be left behind. The ladies and Sister had gathered around the kitchen table. Of course the first topic of conversation was Papa's health. Mrs. Black asked, "How is Walter feeling?" Mama said, "Well, I think he is holding his own. I was worried about his going to get honey this evening but Father assured me he would be okay. I can't help but worry though, he seems so tired lately." Although I worried about Papa I didn't want to hear concerns about his health spoken out loud. If Papa's bad health was not given voice, I could pretend he was okay. Even though I saw him struggle every day, I could pretend all was fine with him if the words were not spoken. "Mama, I am going out to the barn to check on Prince if you don't need me," I said, sure she would say it was okay. Mama smiled and said, "Have you had enough women talk son? Of course you can check on Prince, you might give him a little extra oats. He has been such a good mule of late." Mama might think so but I wasn't too sure. I made my excuses and headed out the kitchen door and to the barn. Talking to Prince was much better than lady talk.

I ran to the oat barrel and raised the lid. Prince began talking to me in mule talk, as he recognized the sound of the lid on the oat barrel. After filling his feed bag, I rubbed Prince behind the ears and he stopped eating long enough to nuzzle the side of my cheek. "Well, old boy," I told Prince, "it's just me and you tonight. The men left me to visit with the girls. I think I will stay in the barn and talk with you." Prince gave me a glance and went back to eating his oats. I put my arms around Prince's neck and said, "Prince, I'm real worried about Papa. He seems so tired most of the time. Sometimes I watch him walk across the yard and he stops every few steps, like he can't catch his breath. But if he sees one of us watching, he just smiles and says *it's nothing, just a little tired today. Tomorrow will be better,* but Prince tomorrow does come and he doesn't seem any better." Prince gave a snort and kept on eating his oats. I felt a little better, just talking about my fears. At least Prince didn't say, it will be oaky, your Papa will get better, when in my heart I knew my worst fears would probably come true. I picked up the pitch fork and went to work, moving new straw into Princes stall so he would have fresh bedding. Work kept my worries at bay.

Brother Finds Himself in a Battle with the Bees

A few hours later, hoots and laughter signaled the *men's* return. Brother was bringing up the rear of the group of bee robbers and did not appear to be feeling quite the grown up man he had been when the bee robbing escapade began. In fact he looked quite mad. He was soaking wet and Grandfather said, "Why, I don't know why that boy decided to go for a swim on a cool night like this." Grandfather continued, laughing, "Why I declare, I don't believe I ever saw that boy run so fast. It seemed old Beelzebub himself was after your Brother." Brother was a little indignant and gave Grandfather a scowl for laughing at him. Brother said, "Well, the bees didn't feel it was cool enough to be real calm about their hive being robbed. Those bees singled me out and chased me right into the creek. Why did they chase me and not you and Papa," Brother asked? "Well", said Grandfather, rubbing his once black beard, now peppered with white and salted with a bit of red here and there. "I believe you might have been a mite scared and those bees knew it." Brother wasn't hurt but his *tail feathers were drooping* a little lower than they had been when he had left for the beginning of the *"bee robbing adventure"*.

His experience reinforced my resolve to stay away from the bees and their trees or hives. I sure love the honey though.

It seemed to be a matter of honor for the Ozarks families to have honey on their table. Mama would not have thought of having a guest for dinner and no honey to go on her biscuits. I still love honey, but mine comes from a gentleman down the road from me, who raises bees and sells honey. I have toyed with the idea of having bee hives, but Brother's experience still lingers in my mind.

Autumn Arrives

Fall was fast approaching. Brother and I were excited about the beginning of the school term. This was little Sister's first year at school and she was apprehensive about attending and leaving Mama and Papa all day. "Brother, will you be there all day with me? Will the teacher like me? Mama, what will you do all day without me?" The questions from Sister went on and on. Finally the big day arrived. Storms had rolled over the hills to the west and the thunder boomed and lighting flashed during breakfast that morning. Mama worried about our crossing Ottery Creek, as Ottery was well known for its flash flooding and raging waters. Papa put his arm around Mama and said to her, "don't worry, the boys can hitch up little Prince and he can take them safely across Ottery Creek." Brother and I were very excited about getting to ride Prince to school the very first day. "Now boys, you be careful and if that water looks to high, don't cross that ford," Papa warned! Brother and I answered that we would be very careful. After all we were entrusted with the care of Sister, a most precious gift in our home.

Mama had prepared a good breakfast with pancakes and salt pork bacon, and mush. We even had a little coffee in our milk that morning. At least Brother and I had coffee. Sister was not yet old enough for that treat. Sometimes we had Postum to drink, but not very often. We usually drank that at Grandmother and Grandfather's house.

We only had about a mile to ride to school and the rain had let up and was now only a drizzle. Brother ran out with his slicker on and brought Prince from the barn. Prince's ears hung low in protest of being led out of the dry barn into the rain. "Come on," Brother called to Sister and me. "Let's go while the rain has let up." Mama fussed over Sister, adjusting the blue bows holding her pig tails. Wisp of red curls crept from the pig tails. Grandmother had ordered a blue rain coat and hat, for Sister to wear to school. Mama helped her put on her coat and hat and kissed her, then kissed me and Brother. "Be careful of the creek," Mama said as a tear slid down her cheek. Her baby was off to first grade. "Maybe we should have them wait until tomorrow to go to school, I'm worried about the high water they must cross to get to school," Mama looked at Papa. "Now Mama, your chicks will be just fine, we must have faith that the Lord is guiding them and little Prince on their way." Papa placed his arm around Mama and smiled at her.

Brother helped Sister up on Prince, and then he swung up behind her. I got the third seat on the back of Prince. Prince trotted down the lane and we held to each other, my arms around Brother as he held Sister. We had only traveled about ½ mile when I glanced back and saw black storm clouds looming over the mountain. "Come on Brother," I yelled. "It looks like another storm is coming." Brother kicked Prince's side, urging him to hurry. The storm hit with a fury, before we reached the creek. "Do you think we should turn back Brother," I shouted over the torrents of rain and the rumble of thunder? I comforted myself with Grandmother's saying that the rumble of thunder was only a potato wagon dumping its potatoes. "No," he shouted back, "I think we can make it over the creek, I can see it ahead and it doesn't appear to be that high yet." Sister was shivering and crying. Brother tightened his grip on her and yelled over a clap of thunder, that we would be okay. Prince balked as we neared the creek's edge, which was out of its banks. Brother urged him on into the water. As we neared the center of creek, I looked up the creek and saw a wall of water, with tree branches and other debris, churning Ottery's usually clear water, now brown with mud, as it roared its way toward the three of us and Prince. "Look out," I shouted as the water began to swirl and wrap around Prince's legs! Prince charged forward, aware of the thundering water racing toward us. Sister began crying and struggling to get away. Brother lost his grip for a second and Sister slipped, dangling in the muddy, raging water. "Grace, hold on to my hand," Brother was now screaming, trying to be heard above the rampaging water. He pulled Sister back onto Prince's back. Prince struggled on, dark water now swirling around his flanks. Just as the brown wall of water had almost reached us, Prince made a final lunge and climbed onto safe ground. Brother urged Prince on as the wall of water was quickly overtaking the bank, on which we had just found safety. Prince struggled up the embankment, just ahead of the water. Our new shoes were water logged and my new pants, clean and ironed when I left home were now very wet and I was sure when they dried they would be caked with mud also. Brother urged Prince to climb higher up the bank which was slippery with all that water and now was breaking away and pieces of the bank were sliding down into the swirling water. Prince stumbled more than once as he fought the slippery slope. "Hold onto Sister Brother shouted over the sound of the water roaring and the thunder clapping." I don't think he heard my reply over the water and Sister's crying. I tried to pat her back, but I couldn't do anything but hold on tight and offer words to her. "Don't cry, it will be okay," I tried to tell her.

Prince Carries Us to Saftey

As soon as we reached higher ground, Brother slid off Prince's back, then he reached up to help Sister down, I followed, shaking with the realization of what a close call we had just had. "We don't have far to go now," Brother comforted Sister, as he wrapped his arms around her. Sobbing, Sister said, choking her words out, "I want to go home! I want my Mama!" "Now Sister Grace, we can't go back across the creek until the water goes down. We are going on to school. The Teacher will have a fire going, as it is a damp, cool day and we can stand by the stove until we dry," Brother patted Sister's shoulder as he spoke. Brother and me patted Prince on the head and checked him over for any cuts or lumps. Prince had escaped the raging flood with only a few scratches.

"Come on let's get back on Prince and get to school before the bell rings," I called to Brother. Brother hoisted little Sister onto Prince's back, and then he swung on. He reached out his hand to me and I climbed back to my usual place, third seat on Prince's back. Off we went down the dirt road, mud splashing on our legs as Prince sloshed down the road, which was now a bed of brown muck.

When we got to school, Teacher met Sister and me at the door of the school house. The school house was built of granite mined from the quarry at Graniteville, just northeast of Ottery Creek. "Why you children are all wet," he said, "come inside and dry by the stove." Sister walked behind me, still shaking with the fear and cold from the early morning first day ride to school. Brother stayed in the school yard and took the bridle off Prince so he could eat grass. Prince knew to wait until school was out and we had climbed on board to head back home. The old Pot Bellied Stove in the middle of the room warmed first our fronts, then our backs, turning our hands bright red. Brother joined us at the stove, after Prince was taken care of.

The room was dim in the storm darkened early morning haze. Mr. Smith, our teacher lit lamps that hung on the wall. It was part of the teacher's job to keep the lamps in working order, filled with coal oil and the wicks trimmed. Parents took turns supplying the wood for the heating of the school during the fall and winter months. The students washed the slate board at the front of the room and did the sweeping. It was always a much sought after chore to be allowed to wash the blackboard. This was usually a position that was allotted to the older boys. Brother might be in line this year to help clean the blackboard.

Sister's sobbing had finally ended, as her interest in the school room took her away from the harrowing experience of the morning. The room contained fifteen desks, with wooden tops and holes for our ink bottles to set in . Benches sat in front of the desks for the smaller students like Sister. In the front of the classroom sat the teacher's desk and a blackboard that took most of the front wall. There was a smell of saw dust and an oil mixture, which was used to clean the wooden floors. We each had a new box of crayons, safely tucked into our coat pockets, and each box had survived the journey. The smell of a new box of crayons always takes me back to Sister's first day of school.

Brother was the hero of the day. Mr. Smith had Brother stand at the front of the class and tell about our adventure of the morning. As I listened, my heart skipped beats and my stomach lurched. With so much excitement, I had failed to realize how close the three of us came to washing away, tumbling and turning down Ottery Creek. I thought of the ghost tale I remembered my Grandmother telling, about a little boy who strayed out of his log cabin, back in the 1880's. She said he had made his way down to Ottery, as the water came roaring out of the hills and down the valley, much as it had this morning. It was believed the water picked the little boy's body up and carried it away, down Ottery to the Black River. His body was never found, but legend has it that on a rainy night, his cries would drift through the hollows and hills, calling *"Mama, Mama,"* sometimes continuing until the rain ceased or daylight crept over Bell Mountain. Children, out at night, strained their eyes, trying to catch a glimpse of the little boy, now just a white vapor, drifting through the night, searching for his home, long since gone. Many people told tales of seeing the small wisp of a boy, floating above the water. Shivers ran down my spine as I thought we might have been carried away, to be with the lost boy forever.

Brother was now telling about Prince having been the real hero of the day. "That little mule strained and pulled against the tree limbs rolling down the creek and high water crashing around us to bring us to safety." "Why I don't believe Mont Black's ole mule *Salty* could have crossed that ford in that high water as well as little Prince crossed it, with the three of us on his back. He struggled, the muddy water reaching his flanks and he was hit with debris that was racing was down the creek. Why he risked his life to save ours." The other students cheered for Prince. I was feeling very proud of Prince that day, the memories of his trips to Aunt and Uncles' farm, when there was work to be done, forgotten for the moment.

Brother had just finished his tale when the door of the school house was flung open and Mama rushed in, her eyes searching for her chicks as she sometimes called her little brood. Papa held her arm to keep her from falling when she saw the three of us safe, as she had become weak from the fear of losing her children to the flood and the sight of us brought such relief. Little Sister ran to Mama and hid her face in Mama's skirt. "Mama, I was so scared, and I told Brother I didn't want to cross that ole creek, but he said it was okay. Mama, I fell off Prince once, but Brother pulled me back and I was all wet and I cried for you. Teacher had me stand by the stove and I dried." The tears were flowing again, as Sister relived her first day of school for Mama, relishing all the hugs and kisses she received. "Prince saved us Mama," Brother and I spoke at the same time. Grandfather and Grandmother had become worried when the storm hit so Grandfather hitched up his wagon and took the path around the mountain to Papa's house. Mama and Papa had jumped into the wagon and left Grandfather and Grandmother at our home. "We took the old road over the mountain so it took us a long time to get here," Papa said. "We asked God to keep the three of you safe. God is good; he answered our prayers and brought our little ones safely to school. Prince will have a nice portion of oats this evening. Mr. Smith, Thank you for caring for our children. It has been an exciting day for little Grace and I think we will take the children home early today, if you would not mind."

Mr. Smith shook hands with Papa and wished us a safe journey home. He stooped and shook sister's hand. "I will see you tomorrow Grace. Hopefully you will arrive at school in a dryer condition than you did today."

"Son," Papa said to Brother, "tie Prince to the wagon and we will go home now." Mama has had enough excitement for the day, haven't you Mama." Mama just smiled and gathered me under her other arm, as Sister was not going to let go of Mama. Brother had Prince tied to the wagon and down the road we went, blankets tucked around us, Sister's exciting first day of school, now becoming a memory.

Grandmother had soup cooking on the stove. We all sat down at the table. Papa asked Grandfather to offer the blessing and thanks was given for our safe return to our family. Of course Brother had to recount our miraculous adventures of the day. Grandmother said we were indeed blessed to have our family safe together on such a day.

After supper, we retired to the parlor and Papa took down his fiddle and Mama sat at the organ, playing some hymns, thankful for the safe return of their children. Papa did not play much anymore as he said it just tired him too much to raise his arms up to hold the fiddle. The sunset spread a rosy glow over the parlor. Mama said she had best light the lamps, as it appeared the sun was being chased away by the twilight.

After a few songs, Papa said it was almost bed time. He opened the Bible, as he did every night. "Tonight I will read about our Savior and his disciples in a storm, much like the three of you were in today, when you were trapped in the raging water of Ottery Creek. Waves rocked the boat, and the disciples called to Christ, *do you not care about us? Do you not care if we drown? Christ rebuked the wind and the wind died down. The water was calm and there was peace. He then said,*

Why are you afraid? Your Mama and me were afraid today and so were you children. But we all prayed and our prayers were answered. When you are afraid, ask God to help you and like today, he will." Papa always knew the right things to say to us, he always made us feel safe. "Now it is bedtime. Tomorrow will come early. Off to bed with all of you," Papa said as he kissed Sister on the cheek.

We climbed the stairs to our rooms, Sister to the little attic room on the left and Brother and I shared the room to the right. Sleep was marred by dreams of the poor little boy who had drowned long ago. He was stretching out his hand to me, ghostly white and cold. I awoke with a start, glancing at the corners of the room. Then I remembered Papa's reading of the Bible story last night, about Jesus on the boat, stretching out his hand and calming the wind. I prayed for God to keep us safe during the night and then I drifted off to sleep.

The smell of coffee perking on the stove and biscuits baking aroused me from a restless night's sleep. "Breakfast is ready," Mama called to us and so started another day of school.

October arrived with the cool, crisp feel of autumn. The hills looked as if an artist had swooped his giant paint brush over the hills, reds, gold, copper, rust, pink and scarlet, a brush stroke here and a drip from the brush there, with the color of the evergreens for contrast, a flick from the brush here and a paint dribble there as the brush glided over our mountains. On and on the brush swooped, circling our valley, turning a sugar maple gold, splashing fire on the sumac that grew along the dry stacked stone fence rows, the stones collected by long forgotten farmers, who were clearing their fields and fencing in their crops with the most plentiful material they had, creek rocks. I could not believe on that morning as the sun rose above Bell Mountain that there could be a more beautiful place in the entire world than our valley was. I have traveled many places since that day, but the beauty of that morning has yet to be matched.

We would be gathering nuts from the hickory and walnut and

hazelnut trees come the weekend, when school was not in session. I preferred the milder taste of the hickory nut to that of the walnut. We had to be very careful in picking out those nut meats as a small piece of shell left in a cookie could cause disaster in ones mouth as you bit down. Mama was very careful with the nuts she used for baking.

We would sell the excess to the little store in Black, located before the road forked, one fork leading to Lesterville and the other fork leading to Centerville, our county seat. Sometimes, if we had a big harvest, buyers of nuts from some other areas, I'm not sure if they were from St. Louis or some other city came and bought the nuts still in the shell. Sometimes in the evenings, when other chores were completed, we picked out nuts meats, as the kernels brought more money than the ones still in the shells did. Other farmers would take their nuts to the store in Black also. We sold sassafras root, blood root and ginseng root. Some we gathered in the spring, like sassafras root. Sassafras had to be dug before the sap rose out of the root. After it was dug, the sassafras would be laid out in the shed to dry, along with ginseng and blood root, tied in bundles hanging from the rafters, ready for sale to the nut and root buyers in the fall. This provided some extra cash for things we needed, like shoes and material for Mama to make our clothes.

I particularly loved the sassafras in the spring. Mama said it thinned our blood, which was good for us after a long winter. Many a cold spring morning would find a steaming pot of sassafras tea on the table. Honey for sweetening was there, but I really favored the tea without the sweet taste. A bottle of root beer brings back the memory of the tea seeping on the stove. Sometimes I will find *Pappy's Sassafras Tea* on the shelf in the supermarket and that is a real treat for me.

Soon it was time for molasses making on Ottery Creek. This was my favorite time of the year, except for Christmas and my Birthday.

All the people living along Ottery and some living in the hills would gather when the sorghum cane was ready for harvest, bringing their cane and families in wagons. Molasses and honey were all the sweeteners we had. The refined white and cane sugars we have today were not common and we could not have afforded them, had they been readily available. The women would bring fried chicken, pies, cakes and other food for the feast. Aunt Maude would always bring my favorite, strawberry-rhubarb pie. Big tables would be set up, made from saw horses and long boards cut at the local sawmill.

Papa, Brother and me had stripped the cane, cut the cane and loaded the wagon with the stripped cane, ready to hitch up Prince and travel the four miles down the road to the Black Farm the next morning. Our seeds were saved from year to year. We carefully removed the seed before the leaves were removed, laying them out to dry for planting the next spring. As we worked, Papa would tell us how our cane seed came from plants our family had raised for over one hundred years. He said his Great Grand Pappy had brought the seeds with him, when he came from West Virginia in a covered wagon. He came over the mountains, just after the Louisiana Purchase. He had settled in the Belleview Valley area. Papa always told us stories about our family history as we worked. As I stripped the leaves from the cane, I thought of my family, one hundred years ago, holding the ancestors of this very cane, peeling the leaves from the cane stalk, much like Papa, Brother and I were doing. Pictures of Papa's Grandma and Grandpa hung in the living room, by the fireplace, but they were old people when the pictures were painted and I often wondered if I looked like Great Grandpa? Many people, who had remembered him, often said my red hair was much like that of my Great Grandpa's. Of course, Sister and I both had red hair. Brother's hair was a light brown.

As Prince was the hero of the valley for bringing Brother, Sister and me to safety during the flood, it was decided he would power the cane mill, along with a more seasoned mule, Jack, who had helped with molasses making for many years. Prince may have been a hero, but he was still a young mule with plenty to learn. I wondered how his being hitched to the mill would set with Prince. Jack, always the lead mule, might have some qualms about playing second fiddle to this contrary little mule. On occasion Prince could still be observed, gazing at Bell Mountain, maybe remembering his lazy days on Aunt and Uncle's farm. Although he had proved to be made of heroic mule stock, I was not convinced of his like for work. Jack had powered the mill first for many years, with a younger mule waiting to stand in when Jack needed a rest. Now Prince would be first mule.

Papa decided Prince needed some training on how to walk in a circle. This training was to be Papa's contribution to our molasses making, as he told Brother and me. "Boys, I doubt that I will be able to feed the cane press this year, so you men will need to do my share of our families work. Now let's start Prince's training on *how* to turn a sorghum mill. We don't want him to upset the *apple cart*, or sorghum mill." Brother put a halter on Prince and clicked, sometimes called a kiss, to signal Prince to begin walking. Brother walked Prince around the pen several times until we felt he had the "hang of walking in a circle."

We were all so excited when the morning for molasses making finally arrived. Mama did not need to call us to breakfast. We were awake before dawn. Papa asked the blessing, and we quickly ate breakfast. Sister helped Mama clear the table and wash the dishes. Papa asked Brother and me to feed Prince, and then hitch him to the wagon. In no time we had Prince hitched up and ready to go. Mama had carried the baskets of food to the wagon and placed the baskets in the back of the wagon. Mama and Sister climbed upon the front seat of the wagon and Brother and I jumped on the back, ready to safeguard the food from any disaster.

Papa, reins in hand called "get up" to Prince. Prince glanced back, and then Prince decided to trot on down the road. We crossed first one, then a second ford on Ottery Creek and started the climb up the hill, then turned down a rocky lane and crossed Ottery Creek for a third time. We rolled our wagon into the Black Family's yard. The frame house stood to the right and a stone barn, made from rock found along Ottery Creek stood in the middle of a field to the left of the house. The stone walls of the barn rose about ten feet and the rest of the wall was made with pine lumber. Wood shingles topped the barn. This barn would with-stand the orneriest mule behavior known to man. Mr. Black raised the big Missouri mules, bred from a draft horse mare and a gigantic Jack. He sold his mules to the Army. His barn was built much like that of Uncle's barn, and both for the same purpose, raising the big Missouri Mules.

I could smell the wood burning on that crisp fall day, ready to cook the cane juice down to make molasses. Victor, one of Mont's sons, ran up to the wagon, "glad you folks are here, come on and I'll lead you to a place to unload the cane and then park the wagon." I jumped off the wagon, ready to help. Brother jumped off the other side of the wagon and hurried to catch up. "Boy, there are a lot of people here, are we late?" Brother was gasping, with the running to catch the wagon, and Papa. Victor said, "No, you're right on time. Of course we can't start the press yet, Prince is the lead mule this year. I get to put in some cane this year," Victor seemed excited as he said this. "Hey, that's great," Brother said as he slapped Victor on the arm. Brother knew how important this was to Victor, as he had missed a lot of school last year with illness and this was the first physical work he would be able to do. His older brothers helped their Father with the farm work, but Victor was too frail to work outside much. Mama had told often of how Victor's Mother, Golda had prayed for Victor, at times not knowing if he would survive. His asthma attacks were not only frightening, but could have been deadly. A few times Mama joined Golda Black, along with some of the other Ottery Creek women, kneeling in the church, praying for God to spare Victor's life and restore his health. Most families could not afford a Doctor in those days, and the nearest Doctor would have been in Ironton, a long buggy ride away. Mama had suggested a tea made with Golden Seal, and Mrs. Black had said more than once, that Mama had saved Victor's life with her teas made with herbs. Mama felt her gift using herbs had been given to her by God.

Long tables had been set up in the yard, and were already groaning with an abundance of food, provided by the ladies of the area. Each lady had brought her specialty and the aroma of the food, yeast bread, fresh baked pies and spiced apples, blended with the wood smoke, combined to sharpen the appetite of a small boy.

Other wagons were pulling into the yard, amid greetings of neighbors, meeting for the first time in weeks. Communication between the people who lived along Ottery Creek, and in the woods and valleys of the area, at times could mean a several mile walk or ride on a mule or horse to a neighbors. Tending crops, laying up food, chopping wood for the winter and making quilts and clothing, and taking care of the farm animals, occupied most of the families time who lived on Ottery Creek, and the infrequent get together, like sorghum making provided opportunities to catch up on each other's families comings and goings.

Mama hugged Aunt and Aunt took Mama's pie from her and carried it to the dessert end of the long table. Of course we saw Aunt and Uncle at the little church we attended each week. It was located along the bank of Ottery, at the head of the lane leading to the cemetery. There the ceremonies of our lives were celebrated. Joys of a new life, dedicated to the Lord, the coming together of a man and woman, to begin a new life together, and the departure of a loved one, some old, some with a life just beginning, all entering this little white clapboard building with a large rock placed at the entrance, to serve as a step. They all would leave this building, either to begin a new life, or travel down the winding dirt road to the Ottery Creek Cemetery.

Children were jumping off wagons as they rolled into the yard, not waiting for the wagons to come to a stop, ready to join their friends at play. Mothers called, "don't get your clothes dirty," almost a required warning, as their children charged off to engage in activities that required a certain amount of dirt. A large hill at the side of the house made a perfect place to roll down. Shoes and socks were tossed aside, as we braved the cold, spring fed Ottery Creek. There were rocks to turn over and crawdads to catch to chase the girls with. The girls would run, pretending to be scared, screaming, as they fled from the crawdad pinchers clacking, as they waved in the air, hopelessly grabbing for something to hang onto. We knew the girls were not really afraid, as they had caught as many of the bug-eyed creatures as the boys had.

There were bluffs to scale, trees to climb and the very best activity, arrow head hunting. Pre-historic mounds dotted the hillsides to the East of Ottery Creek. If I were lucky, an arrow head or two might be found today. Papa had found a black axe head as he was plowing a field two springs ago. Papa said these artifacts were from the Woodland Era. These people lived on this land twelve hundred years ago. Papa loved to share the history of our land, often telling stories to Brother, Sister and me after supper, of the Woodland Inhabitants, followed by the Osage many centuries later. Sometimes he spoke of our ancestors, the Scotch-Irish, who came from back East by way of Kentucky and Tennessee.

Then the molasses making began. Our play time had ended. Papa called Brother and me to help with the making of molasses. Little sister continued to play with the other girls but we had *man's work*, to do. When the cooking time came we would be free to run and play again. Brother was ready to attach the boom to Prince's trace chains and the tight rein was attached to the lead pole. Papa checked Brother's work, giving advice here and there. The lead pole would take Prince in a circle to turn the cane press. Three rollers would turn as Prince walked in his circle. The extracted juice would pour into a thirty gallon bucket, ready to pour into the juice pan, which could hold one hundred gallons of juice from the cane. The left over cane stalk would be pressed out the left side of the press.

My job, along with two other boys would be to haul the cane stalk that had been pressed and the juice removed, away from the mill.

Brother Feeds the Cane into the Press

Later, this would be ground into fodder for the livestock. Brother would get to take Papa's place this year, feeding our cane into the press. Papa was still feeling poorly and the men in the family were responsible for this step in the molasses making. Brother was quite proud of himself, as he stepped forward to feed our cane into the press when it came our family's time to use our cane. Brother stood very tall as he began to feed the cane into the mill, one stalk at a time. It took about an hour to empty our wagon of our cane. Mr.

Black and another man carried our bucket of cane juice to the pan that had been placed over the fire. Papa sat in a wooden, straight back chair. He patted Brother on the back when our cane was finished and told him he was so proud of him. Brother may have been tired after pressing the cane, but he sure looked like he had found a million dollars when Papa praised him in front of all the other boys and men.

Prince worked for several hours, then he was unhooked and I led him down to the creek for a drink, and then gave Prince some grain from a bucket in the back of our wagon. A hug around Prince's neck was certainly called for as he did his job without turning over the press or running away or stealing any of the farmers straw hats. I breathed a sigh of relief. My nightmares had held impending disaster for the future of molasses for the Ottery Creek people for the winter. Disaster had been averted and now a more seasoned molasses maker, Jack, Uncle's mule would finish the press work.

Now the work of skimming the molasses began. As the juice bubbled, two men at a time skimmed the juice, removing the foam with large skimmers with long wooden handles. Good natured calls would ring out, "do you need relief yet?" This was hot work even on a brisk fall day. It was a badge of honor to be the man who skimmed the longest.

I glanced at Papa, sitting, talking with some of the older men, too old or sick for the hard work of molasses making. At first glance Papa seemed happy, but on closer examination, he seemed to have a slump in his shoulders and his eyes were ringed with dark circles. I very seldom ever really looked at Papa, he was just there, always kind, always my Papa. But on that day I really looked at him and even at ten years old, I was seeing for the first time, a frail, old man. The sun was shining down on me, but I felt as if ice water had been poured down the back of my neck.

I was beginning to feel the rumblings of hunger when Sara

Maude, one of Mont's daughters rang the dinner bell. The men, including Brother, as he had taken Papa's place this year loading the cane into the mill, would be first in line for dinner. Brother had already lined up at the pump to wash his hands and splash water on his face. He seemed to be quite full of himself, standing there with all the men, while I was still in the children's category. I kept an eye on the fried chicken and the rhubarb pie, as I was scared it would all be gone before my turn came. At last, I was close to the table, but only after the girls had their plates full. It seemed to me the ten year old boys were always the last in any line. Much to my relief, there was plenty of chicken, gravy, mashed potatoes and rhubarb pie left. Brother and I chose a seat under a large oak, brilliant with red, green, gold and brown leaves.

As we finished eating, one of the Latham girls brought out her banjo, followed by several men, bringing guitars from their wagons. Mr. Lewis was the master fiddle player in the valley. He sometimes played at dances on Saturday night, and he now began to tune up his fiddle. He drew his bow across the rosin several times, and then struck up a tune. The children ran up the hill, tired of their play but ready to do a jig or two. Warren Black was learning the fiddle, and he took a break from the skimming to join in, ready to learn a thing or two from Mr. Lewis. Several of the men began to jig dance, a dance handed down from their Scottish Ancestors. Soon some of the ladies joined and then a square dance began.

Brother was still skimming, but I could see his foot tapping and I could tell he was ready for relief. Brother did love to dance, even at twelve years old. I really didn't care much for the idea as it meant I would need to have my arm around a girl and at the young age of ten, girls did not appeal to me. If I were teased about a girl, I would scrunch up my face in a disgusted look. How Grandfather loved to tease me. He said my freckles all joined together when I scrunched my face and I had a red colored nose. Of course I liked to peek at the little dark haired girl with the pig tails, dancing a jig from time to time, but I sure didn't want anyone to know about that.

Brother called, "the bubbles are as big as silver dollars, and I believe the molasses are ready." Papa and Grandfather came to look as I heard Grandfather tell Papa, "that boy may just want to go dancing and the molasses may not be cooked." But sure enough they pronounced the molasses making complete and the buckets could be filled.

Mama and Mrs. Black stood at the back of the line to fill their buckets with hot molasses. Mama never liked to *push herself,* as she would say, and I am sure her friend Golda felt the same way. I hurried over, quite sure there would not be enough left for us. "Mama, shouldn't you and Mrs. Black move toward the front of the line? We want to be sure there is enough left for us," I complained. Mama tousled my hair with her free hand. "Son, there will be enough for all of us. Patience is a virtue you will need to learn. Pushing in front does not mean more for us. What if we all pushed and shoved? The molasses could all be spilled, then the hard work the men did would be lost. Don't worry; we will have our share of the molasses." This gave me little comfort at the time, but there was little I could do but shuffle my feet and wait.

After the molasses was ladled into the buckets of the waiting ladies, each child would be given a homemade roll, left over from lunch, and we would be allowed to dip it into the remainder of the molasses left after all the buckets had been filled. As Brother was in the *man* category this year, he did not get to participate in this treat. This was just like a trip to the candy store for children now-days. Of course I had never participated in that particular treat of a trip to a candy store; molasses drippings were as close as most of the children from Ottery Creek had come to a candy store.

Mama made fudge for Christmas and cookies and divinity. After Christmas, about Valentine's Day someone would have a taffy pull.

I did get a scoop of ice cream last summer, when Grandfather took Brother, Sister and me to the store at Ironton and allowed us to purchase a cone. What a treat on a hot day. I can still see Sister, her little face hot, with perspiration dotting her nose, along with a sprinkling of freckles. The strawberry ice cream ran down the side of her cone as she hurriedly licked the cone, not wanting to lose a single drop of the cold, pink treat. The molasses drippings were a great treat to the children, as sweets were a rare thing.

The dancing continued, along with trips back to the left-over food on the table. Dusk was beginning to fall on the dancers. You could see a harvest moon, beginning to rise over Bell Mountain. Papa said the moon would light our way home, but we had better be going. Papa looked very tired, but he protested that he felt fine. Mama gathered up her pots and dishes. Goodbyes were shouted to everyone. Papa asked Brother if he would like to drive the wagon home. A tired Prince was hooked up to the wagon. It appeared he was too worn out to participate in any mischievous behavior on his way home. Prince trotted down the lane leading to Ottery Creek. Up the road we went. We were all tired, but I noticed Papa leaned on Mama's shoulder. Even to a ten year old boy, he looked exhausted. A cough shook his body and Mama pulled a blanket she had draped around him more tightly.

"Look," Mama called, there is the Big Dipper, and it pours its water to the North, over the two stars at the top of the Dipper. There's the little dipper, and Sister, there is the constellation Leo. That's your birth sign. Papa, don't you think Grace looks a bit like that new golden kitten Aunt has. We shall have to ask her to name that kitten Leo." Papa smiled and said; "indeed" he thought Sister looked just like a golden kitten. Perhaps we should call her *kitten* from now on. Sister was getting sleepy and just a bit cranky by this time. "No, you will not call me kitten, I am not a cat," she quarreled. Papa laughed and said, "No, little one, you are not a kitten at all, you are a very pretty little girl, so we will not call you kitten." Why if you were a kitten you would need to lap up your milk from a saucer instead of drinking your milk from a cup."

Satisfied, Sister drifted off to sleep. Mama carried Sister into the house when we arrived home. Brother and I unhitched Prince and put him into the barn. "I believe you deserve some extra oats and hay tonight Prince. You were such a good little mule today," I said as I rubbed behind Princes' ears. Brother said, "Will you get the oats and hay?" I'll bring Prince a fresh bucket of water." After feeding Prince and shutting the barn door, Brother and I walked back to the house. A warm glow from the lamps Mama had lit flowed from the kitchen windows. We saw the lamp at the front of the house, in Papa and Mama's bedroom go dark. "I believe this was a hard day for Papa," Brother said as he draped his arm across my shoulder and we walked back toward the house without saying another word.

A Pig Hunting We're Going

A few days later, Grandfather and Grandmother pulled up in their wagon. Grandfather helped Grandmother down from the wagon and with a wave she hurried into the house, caring a box of goodies. Grandmother never came without some treats for us. "Boys," Grandfather called to Brother and me as we came out of the barn. "You're Grandmother and I came over for a pig catching party. It's getting that time of the year. Tomorrow evening we'll head down to the north end of the road to the cemetery. I saw signs of a hog wallow or two up in the woods. I expect we will find our hogs up there. One evening last week I was up that way and saw a site just like a site my Grand-Pappy showed me when I was a little boy. He said the wild hogs came from the hogs early settlers brought here in the 1700's. The hogs reproduced and spread over the country side. I didn't think I would ever see something like that again. I'm anxious to show you boys a hog bedding down like you could never have imagined. But never mind, I want you to see for yourselves. Come tomorrow evening we'll head out and track down those hogs. Then you will see what I'm talking about," Grandfather exclaimed, excited about the next evening! Then the next few days, we'll work on the hog pen. I don't want your Papa wearing himself out, so we'll get the work done ourselves. Does that sound alright to you boys?" It seemed we were all watching out for Papa these days. Even little Sister would pull a quilt over Papa's legs if it slipped to the floor as we sat in the parlor in the evenings, saying, "Papa, you don't want to get a chill," sounding much like Mama or Grandmother did when they talked to Papa.

When we returned from school the next day, Grandfather had the hog pen almost completed. Grandfather was outside when we came down the lane. He called to us, "what do you think boys, will that hold a couple of little pigs?" We ran to where Grandfather was leaning on the post at the corner of the pen. "Why I think we could hold five or six pigs in there," I said as I climbed up the side of the pen. "Well at least four or five," Brother offered. Grandfather had completed the pen in record tie. It seemed he was ready to track down those hogs. Sister had stood listening to us, but she tired of the conversation about hogs and ran into the house. When we came into the kitchen, she was already setting the table and Mama and Grandmother were moving food from the wood cook stove to the table. A long pine table sat in the center of the kitchen, much too big for our usual five people. Papa had made this table for Mama when she found Brother would be making his arrival into their home. I think Papa envisioned many sons and daughters sitting around the table, with him at the head and Mama at the other end. He had to settle for the three of us. He always seemed to think we were blessings and never acted as if he felt cheated.

Grandfather was sure in a hurry, "come along boys and finish your supper," he said as Brother and I were still eating our supper and perhaps taking a tad too long. "We need to get started before it gets dark and the days are not as long now as the days of summer were." I couldn't imagine what he was in such an *all fired hurry for.* Mama would correct me if I said that expression out loud. It was new to me, learning it from the older boys at school. I enjoyed letting those words roll around in my head. Mama would let me know when I slipped up and uttered those words. She felt I was only a step away from cussing. I now knew better than to say it in front of Mama or Papa. Brother and I scarfed down the last few bites and hurried to put on our coats and boots. Grandfather was already outside waiting. "Let's go boys," he said as he headed down the path, lantern in hand, in case we didn't return before dark.

Grandfather kept a fast pace, as he was long legged. Brother and I had to jog to keep up with him. Finally, he slowed and turned to us, pressing a finger against his lips, "Boys, keep real quite now, we don't want to scare them off." We climbed up a small bluff that over looked a narrow ravine. All of a sudden we heard them, hogs grunting and sniffing and squealing. The big boars came first, rooting around in the leaves, scooping out a place as they lay down. Next came the mama pigs, the big sows, grunting and rooting the leaves with their snouts, plopping down on top of the boars, and covering themselves with leaves. Last to arrive were the shoats and piglets, squealing in their high pitched voices, lying on top of the other hogs, tossing more leaves from the forest floor. When all had quieted and settled down for the night, all you could see was a huge circle of leaves. Not one tail or snout was left uncovered. The pigs had vanished from our site.

We hurried home as the darkness was settling over us like a blanket of soft black lamb's wool, and although Grandfather had brought a lantern we liked to be home before the darkness of night enveloped us. The moon and stars were hiding behind a blanket of clouds that could spell an early snow fall. Winter was fast approaching.

"Come along boys, tomorrow is Saturday and we will bring a couple of piggies home, come daylight," Grandfather chuckled. Down the lane Grandfather jigged, singing the nursery rhyme, *to market, to market to buy a fat pig, home again, home again, jiggety-jig.*"

Papa and Mama came to the door to see what the ruckus was about. Grandmother was standing behind them and when she saw Grandfather jigging, she scoffed, "why he's just showing off. He's very proud of his ability to still dance." Sometimes Grandmother felt Grandfather acted to childish. Her *rheumatiz*, as she called it had left her knees stiff and she couldn't dance anymore. I had heard that she and Grandfather had been the best dancers at barn raisings and other dances.

After we came in and warmed ourselves by the fireplace, Papa brought out the Bible and read the scripture versus for the evening. We said our prayers and hurried up to bed, as we had an adventure coming in the morning.

Brother and I awoke to a terrible racket coming from the bottom of the stairs. We tumbled of bed at about the same time, almost colliding! We ran down stairs boots in hand. There was

Grandfather, banging on the bottom of a pot with a big spoon. "Hurry up boys, the pigs will be out of bed before we get there and we need to catch a couple of the little ones before the sows decide not to part with their babies. I want to catch the pigs before the sows and boars roust about. We must be fast, as those hogs can become ferocious if we try to take their little ones." Grandfather hurried us to a waiting breakfast. We scarfed down a few bites and headed out the door, pulling on our coats and wrapping our scarves around our necks as we went. "Now boys, bundle up as it is a very cold morning," Mama warned. Grandfather had Prince hitched to an old wooden sled we had used to pull firewood from the trees we had cut along the creek bank. Grandfather was carrying a bucket of slop or pig bait, as he called the leftovers from our meals during the past week. He had some rope and several large grass sacks, or gunny sacks, as some called the sacks feed came in. These sacks had great value on our farm. The most important use of those sacks to me was to cover the ice in the old crank ice cream maker, on the rare occasion when Grandfather and Grandmother had ice to make ice cream in the summer. Ice cream making only happened one time that I can remember. Ice was scarce in the summer. Our only refrigeration was the spring branch. Down the road went Grandfather, leading Prince with his halter, as Prince pulled the sled. Brother and I jogged along beside the sled. In the hour just before the sun broke over Bell Mountain, jutting out of the darkness, a faint glimmer of light, shadowed by the mountain, forecasted the day to come. The clouds had broken and we had just enough moonlight left from the night, to make our way without the lantern light.

Grandfather held up his hand and stopped Prince a short distance from the pigs. He took his slop bucket and emptied the contents on the trail in front of us. The bucket contained the foul smelling food of our meals from the past week. Grandfather led Prince out of sight of the trail. Grandfather called, "get ready boys, we must be quick. When the pigs come snorting around the slop, I'll put one in my sack and you boys grab the next pig. Throw the bag on the sled and be ready to run from those mama pigs."

We hid in some scrub brush on the side of the trail and waited. It didn't take long before we heard some stirring in the hog bed. The sounds were quieter than last night. Maybe the pigs were not too anxious to leave their warm bed. At last a few little pigs came trotting down the trail. They held their little snouts to the air, then came running. We could hear the rumblings of the larger hogs, but they were plumper and slower than the little ones. Grandfather hollered, "grab one boys, I'll catch that one at the back." Off Grandfather ran to grab a pig. Brother and I followed suit, I caught the legs of a medium sized pig and Brother stuffed him into the sack. What a ruckus they raised. Grandfather had his sack thrown on the sled. "Hurry boys, those old sows will be after us soon. Brother and I threw our sack on the sled and hopped on. Grandfather clicked to signal Prince to hurry. For once Prince didn't balk. I think he sensed the danger lurking behind us. Brother looked back and screamed at Grandfather "here they come and their running real fast!" Grandfather picked up his pace. "Hang on boys," he cried. Looking back I could see the hogs stopping at the pile of slop Grandfather had thrown in the middle of the trail. "I think they've stopped," I yelled at Grandfather again. "Not for long," Grandfather replied, "it will only take a minute for those hogs to clean up that slop. We're not out the woods yet." On down the path went Grandfather, with the little pigs, bouncing, tied in their sacks on the sled behind Prince as he raced toward home. Brother and I ran beside the sled and we didn't slow until we saw the smoke from our chimney twisting upward into the cold morning air. Then we slowed to a trot.

Putting the Pigs in Grass Sacks

When we finally reached the pig pen, Grandfather was out of breath. "Get those pigs into the pen," Grandfather gasped. "Don't untie the sacks until you are in the pen with the gate closed. After all that work, we don't want to chase those pigs again." Grandfather made sure the gate was secure and Brother and I ran into the house.

"Ida Red," Grandfather called as we came into the kitchen from the back porch. Grandmother's name was Ida and when she was young, Mama said Grandmother's hair had been red, much like Sister's and my hair. Grandmother came slapping a dish cloth at Grandfather, "what do you want now," she asked? Grandmother acted annoyed when Grandfather called her Ida Red, but I think she really enjoyed his nickname for her. "Why Ida, breakfast was a long time ago and these boys and I have worked up quite an appetite catching pigs this morning. Do you think you could find us something to eat as dinner time is quite a way off and I don't think I can last much longer," Grandfather gave Grandmother his most winning smile. "Well, we have some biscuits and buttermilk. How does that sound to you boys," Grandmother asked? Brother and I allowed that would be right tasty. We pulled our chairs up to the table, just as Papa came into the kitchen. "Was your pig catching expedition successful," Papa asked? Without waiting for an answer, Papa reached for the biscuits and said, "Mother Ida, would you pour me a glass of that buttermilk?" "Why of course John," Grandmother smiled. I think we all smiled, happy to see Papa with an appetite that morning. He seldom did more than move his food from one side of his plate to the other side.

We were just taking our plates from the table to the dish pan when little Sister popped into the kitchen. "Did you catch some little pigs," Sister asked? Grandfather gave me and Brother a knowing look, as if to say, watch her so she doesn't get too attached. Brother took charge saying, "Sister, we'll go out and look at the pigs, but no petting, that could be dangerous and no naming the pigs. Just remember they will be bacon on our plate."

Sister wrinkled up her nose and said she knew all that and she would not be making pets out of the pigs, she just wanted to take a look. Brother and I exchanged glances. We had our work cut out for us as Sister could be quite determined for a little five year old girl. I think that came from Sister being the baby and quite spoiled to boot.

Cute Little Pigs

Pig in a Pen

Sister ran out to the pig pen with Brother and me right behind. Up on the fence she went and called to Brother and me, "oh look at that cute little tail, see how it curls! I think we should call him Curly and the other one Lawrence, don't you?" "Now Sister Grace," Brother said in his most grown up voice, "we talked about this at breakfast, don't you remember? These pigs will be our meals this winter. No naming, no petting! Now get inside before I tell Papa and Mama." Sister stuck out her lower lip, however, she went inside like Brother asked her to, stomping her feet along the way.

School kept the three of us busy. It wasn't long before the time came to butcher the pigs. They had grown quite plump on the corn and slop we fed them. I must admit, I didn't look forward to butchering time. Those little pigs were really cute. I just needed to *buck up* as Brother called it. Thinking about *bucking up* from an adult point of view meant ignoring feelings, pushing feelings to the back of one's mind. That is what Brother and I did. I wondered if Papa, Mama and Grandfather and Grandmother had to do that also.

Papa planned to butcher this week as the weather was cold enough. Some of the neighbors would come to help as butchering two hogs was quite labor intensive. Wagons pulled into the yard just after daybreak. Mama and Grandmother had breakfast ready and all joined in. The huge granite coffee pot was on the stove, ready for a large crowd. The neighbor ladies joined Mama and Grandmother, dishing up the food. Several men were in the yard, filling large barrels with water from the hand pump in the yard and building fires under the barrels. When the water was just right, the hog's bodies would be lowered into the barrels for a short time to loosen the hair. Then came the scraping, which fell to Brother and me. I really didn't like this job. Working fast was the key to success, as the hair had to be removed quickly or it would set again. Warren and Marvin Black would be helping scrape the hair from the pig's skin. I don't think they liked the job any more than Brother or I did. It was a very cold morning, quite necessary for the preservation of the meat. Our hands would be red and sore, first from the hot water and then from the cold air.

I heard the first shot, then another. No squeals accompanied the shots. That meant it had been a good kill and the pigs had died instantly. The pigs would be hoisted onto a beam. The throats would be cut so the pigs could be bled out. The pigs would be hanging upside down. It took two men to hoist those pigs up into the air. Then, of course would come the scalding and scraping.

After the pigs had been killed I could go outside. I might be a country boy, but the killing of animals was something I tried to avoid. I know this made me seem different from many of my schoolmates, who tromped through the hills hunting squirrel and rabbit after school and on weekends. Many of the families in our area survived on wild game. Mama and Grandmother killed the chickens and Grandfather and Papa took care of the other meat. Of course I never objected to eating the meat.

The hogs would be split open and the intestines would be dropped into a waiting pan. The ladies would cut the fat off the intestines, along with the fat from other areas of the hog, to make lard. Then they would clean the intestines to stuff with sausage. Grandfather cut out the bladders and handed Brother and me each one. "Blow these up and you boys can play ball. Brother and I looked at each other. Brother raised the end of the bladder to his lips and blew. Not to be outdone, I did the same. Soon we each had a fine ball. Sister came out of the house about that time and Brother tossed her the ball, yelling "catch!" Sister caught the ball, but soon realized what she had in her hand. Into the house she ran screaming. We didn't have much time to relish our prank or get into trouble. It was time to go to work. The first hog was being dipped into the hot water. The hog was hoisted from the barrel of hot water and placed on a long wooden table, sat up for the scraping. "Come on boys, it's time to get busy," Grandfather said, as he handed out the scrapers. Scraping hogs was a fast paced work. The Black Brothers joined Brother and me and we worked fast, trying to remove the hair before it set. After the insides of the pig had been carefully cleaned, it would be hung to *let out the body heat.* This would require overnight hanging. Some of the neighbors who lived close would go home, but several families would camp out on mats on the floor. That would mean some singing, with Mama playing the organ and a couple of guitar players. We would all turn in early. Brother and I slept on a mat as our room was occupied by Mr. and Mrs. Black and Sister's room housed Grandfather and Grandmother. We hurried off to sleep as we would be out in the cold early the next morning, cutting up the pigs and making sausage.

We were all too tired to have much music on that night. Mama played a couple of songs on the organ and Grandfather brought out his old guitar. Uncle Latham had brought along his guitar and both played along with Mama. Papa then read a few Bible verses and

Grandfather said the evening prayer. Rather he sang the prayer, *If I have wounded any soul today, if I have caused someone to go astray, if I have walked in my own willful way, Dear Lord forgive.* This has always been one of my favorite songs and I never hear it anymore, but how fitting the words are. I can still hear Grandfather's rich baritone voice singing Dear Lord, forgive. I believe the name of the song is *An Evening Prayer.*

Morning dawned bright and cold. "The perfect day for cutting up the meat and hanging it in the smoke house," Grandfather said. If our fingers and toes don't freeze off, I thought. A long wooden table had been set up on the back porch and the men lined up on both sides of the table to slice the meat. Mama, Grandmother and the other ladies were removing the fat from the meat and placing it in a cast iron pot to render lard. Mrs. Black stirred the kettle, now and then, dipping off the grease. White lard kept better than brown lard and removing the grease was the key to having white lard.

The sausage mill stood ready and Uncle was cutting a mix of lean meat and fat to get just the right mix for the ladies to make sausage. Grandmother added sage to her sausage. We all worked until the meat was hanging in the smoke house and the hickory chips were smoking in a pit next to the smoke house. The smoke house drew in the smoke, acting as a chimney. The meat would be smoked for five or six days. It would then hang in the smoke house, ready for eating. We would have pig tongue tonight, and that was a real treat. The hogs heads and other pieces of the meat were boiling in a pot and Mama and Grandmother would make head cheese the next day. We all worked until all the meat was processed. Tired friends and neighbors gathered in the kitchen to share a meal of fresh pork before they started home. Next week we would be at another neighbors, helping with another butchering, until all the smoke houses in the valley were full of meat for the winter. Papa was completely worn out and said he would go to bed before evening prayers and asked

Grandfather to read the scripture and have prayer that night and we all retired early.

Fall was beginning to turn to winter. Thanksgiving that year was quite. Only Grandfather and Grandmother came a few days before Thanksgiving and would eat Thanksgiving Dinner with us. Grandmother would help with the preparations. In the past we had gone to Aunts and Uncles for a great feast. Cousins from the city would be there. Music would be played after dinner and continue into the night. The children would become tired and would head up to the attic of Aunt's house. Straw ticks were already spread on the floor, waiting for the youngsters to sleep on. Of course, ghost stories of the poor little drowned boy would be told and retold. I really didn't want to hear that story again, because that could have been me.

Mama thought all the crowd would be too much for Papa, as he had become much frailer this year. He tired much more easily and many evenings would find him in bed, just before the darkness began to settle over the house and barn.

Mama had made pumpkin pie, from pumpkins stored in the cellar, and my favorite, hickory nut pie. Nowadays pecan pie is all the rage for Thanksgiving, but I would love to taste just one piece of my Mama's hickory nut pie. There were also gooseberries in the cellar and so as not to disappoint Grandfather, Mama made a gooseberry pie also. Grandfather had killed a wild turkey a few days before, taking his rifle to the woods, and had a successful hunt. The turkey was dressed and hanging in the smoke house, ready for transport to the oven. We would also have dressing with sage from Mama's herb garden, just outside the kitchen door. It had been growing there for as long as I could remember and Mama cut stems from the sage plant and hung them in the kitchen from a beam nailed to the wall. Mama said she and Papa had planted her "kitchen garden," as she called her herb garden, the spring after she and Papa married.

Grandfather and Grandmother had made a trip to Ironton and purchased celery. We only had celery twice a year, at Thanksgiving and Christmas. The rest of the time, Mama would cook with celery seed. The smells of the celery and onions cooking for the dressing, mixed with the smell of yeast rolls and pies still drifts through my memory, especially at Thanksgiving and Christmas.

I missed the cousins, but we had a wonderful Thanksgiving. Grandfather read the Scripture and offered Thanks. I thought he would never finish, I could hear my stomach rumbling. Sister was swinging her legs under the table, impatient. I saw Mama reach over and place her hand on Sister's arm, a signal to set still. Finally Grandfather finished, and said amen. Papa said, "Pa," that is what he called Grandfather, "why don't you carve the turkey this year, seeing it was you that provided the turkey for the table." Grandfather, holding the carving fork and knife, carved with great waves of his arms. Grandmother told him someone was going to lose a nose, as wildly as he was swinging that carving knife. Grandfather said, "I am an experienced turkey carver, and never has a nose been sacrificed when I carved the turkey."

We passed our plates to Grandfather and he forked a piece of turkey on each plate. As the meal was completed, stomachs full to running over, we each took our plates to the sink, where Mama filled the dish pan with hot water from the stove. Mama and Grandmother washed the dishes while Brother and I dried. Grandfather and Papa retreated to the parlor. Papa rubbed his arm and shoulder, but when Grandfather asked him if he was okay, he smiled and said, "After a fine meal like your daughter and her Mama cooked, all is right with the world."

After the kitchen was put right, we joined Papa and Grandfather in the parlor. Grandfather told stories of Thanksgivings when he was young. He also told stories about Mama and how she met Papa. Mama blushed as Grandfather told how Papa had courted Mama for quite some time before she consented to marry him. She had taught school before she met Papa. Grandfather had been the county clerk in Iron County before he became old. He said he rode his mule or took a buggy into Ironton each day, returning home after dark. Grandfather and Grandmother lived in Iron County and we, living just down the road, but on the other side of the county line, were residents of Reynolds County.

Some of our cousins stopped by for a visit after dinner. They were on their way back to St. Louis. They visited for a spell but they could tell too much conversation wore Papa out, so they cut their visit short. Most of the city cousins had automobiles by that time. We still had our wagon and Prince as our mode of transportation. Of course Grandpa had an automobile, but it was only used on special occasions. Mules and buggies offered a more reliable way of getting from pace to place in our *neck of the woods*, due to muddy, deep ruts in the roadway, during the wet months of the year. In the very hot summer the road beds would become a light brown powder, like the scorched corn starch, Mama would make in the summer, to treat our chaffed skin. The light brown powder would sift over the mule, wagon or buggy and all of the occupants. In the summer we preferred to walk, if the distance was not too far. Only our feet would become a dusty brown when we walked.

As we gathered back in the parlor that evening, after eating some leftovers, Papa said, "Mother, why don't you read the story of the first Thanksgiving." "Sister, would you bring me the story of the pilgrims from the bookshelf in the hall," Mama asked? I saw Sister peer into the dark hall and she didn't make a move to get the book. "Come on Sister, I will help you find the book," Brother said. Together they went into the hall, carrying the lamp from the table. Soon Sister returned bearing the book, and handed it to Mama. Mama began to read, "The first Thanksgiving was celebrated in Plymouth, Massachusetts in the year 1621. About one hundred and one men, women and children had made the trip form Holland. They had originally left England and went to Holland.

They wanted to separate from the Church of England. They sailed over the Atlantic Ocean, a very long, dangerous trip and came to the area they called Plymouth. An Indian named Squanto helped the settlers. He could speak English as he had been kidnapped and made a slave in Europe. He had learned English and made his way back to America only to find his family dead. She continued, not quite reading just telling the story we had heard for many Thanksgivings. "The Pilgrims didn't have enough food to last the winter, but the Wampanoag Indians came to the Pilgrims rescue. They taught the Pilgrims how to plant food and how to fish. Mama recalled, "I remember a picture of the Indians showing the Pilgrims how to put a fish in a hole with their seeds, to fertilize the plants." "They had a bountiful harvest that year and the Indians and Pilgrims gathered to have a three day celebration." Mama continued to tell the story. "What foods do you think the first Thanksgiving included, children," Mama asked?" I guessed turkey. Mama said "I don't think so, but maybe they shot a wild turkey." "What other foods do you think they had," Mama questioned? Sister exclaimed, "at least ten hundred pumpkin pies," her eyes aglow at the thought of so many pumpkin pies, all in one place, and all at one time. "Well maybe," Mama said. Brother, sure of his facts from other Thanksgiving stories said "cranberries." "You are correct," Mama smiled, "at least that is what our book says, and cranberries would have grown wild in that part of the country." "Our book says they also had corn and deer meat." Mama looked at Papa, who had dozed off to sleep. "Children, I believe Thanksgiving and all the pies have tired your Papa," Mama said softly as she placed a kiss on Papa's forehead. "Papa, it's time to say goodnight. I believe the children are tired and I am all tuckered out. It has been a good day, hasn't it Grandma?"

Grandmother agreed that indeed it had been a most wonderful

Thanksgiving. "God has provided well for us this year. Why we are all together and certainly had plenty to eat and not just today but all year long." Grandmother continued, telling of a winter when her Father had taken ill and she and her sisters were small. "Father had not been able to hunt or fish, so meat was very scarce. We were thankful for what we had, but I do believe we lived on cow peas that winter. I really don't like cow peas to this day," Grandmother continued with a laugh. Grandmother and Grandfather slept in Sister's bed in the winter time, when they visited and Sister slept on a folding cot, next to Grandmother. Grandmother said sleeping in the same bed with Sister was like sleeping with a wild cat. She rolls and kicks and heavens only know what else when she sleeps. Grandmother said she thought the cot was a wonderful addition to our home.

We all went up the stairs to our rooms. Brother pulled up his covers, ready for sleep, but I was ready for conversation. "Brother," I said, "do you think Papa is really sick?" After a long pause, Brother answered, "well, I think we should keep an eye on him and not let him work very hard. If we see him working, we need to step in and take over. Maybe with rest he will get stronger. Mama brews some powerful teas. If that doesn't fix him, it's likely nothing will, but I believe he will get better come spring and warm weather. Just remember, if you see him trying to pick something up, or do work, step in and do it for him. But most of all we need to say our prayers for him." I vowed I would watch over Papa and take work from him when I could. I kept talking, but no answer came from Brother's side of the room. A soft snore was all I could hear. Soon his snoring became fainter and fainter and I drifted off to sleep and good dreams.

December brought much whispering and secrets around our house. Brother began spending much of his free time in the shed behind the house. "Now I am warning both of you," Brother said firmly, to Sister and me. **DO NOT COME NEAR THE SHED UNLESS I INVITE YOU!** Mama and Papa have given me the shed for the entire month, and you both are banned." Of course we knew something was afoot. I began a devious plan to see in the window. The window was very high above my head, on the east side of the shed. At first I stacked some wooden boxes, and climbed upon them, but Sister saw me and hollered at me, "What are you doing on those boxes, Brother?" Of course the boxes tumbled down and so did I, making such a racket that Brother, Mama and Papa came running. "My goodness, are you hurt," asked Mama? "No he's not hurt, just look at him, he's not hurt at all!" He's just trying to peek into the window, after I asked him not to look in the shed! I told him to stay away," Brother fumed! "Why can't he just do what he is told," he continued? "Now, Now," Papa said, "what if I had told you to stay away from the shed and indicated that a secret was unfolding under you're very eyes, only don't look. What would you have done?" Brother just hung his head as he said, "I just wanted a surprise for Brother and Sister." I was sorry I had caused a problem, but I still wanted to find out what was going on in that shed.

A few days passed and my curiosity grew stronger. I heard sawing and hammering every evening after we came home from school. Finally I could stand it no longer. I figured I could see inside the shed if I climbed onto Prince's back. I put a halter on Prince and led him out of the barnyard, and up to the side of the shed. I swung my leg over Prince, and then proceeded to stand on his back. Standing on his back was just too much for that little mule. He began braying and bucking, all at the same time. I landed in a snow drift, unhurt but shaken. Brother came out of the shed, his face crimson, and Papa and Mama came out of the house. Papa was not happy with me at all. "I thought we had agreed that Brother was working on a Christmas surprise and you would not snoop, and here I find you on the ground. You could have been badly hurt. What were you doing with Prince out here?" Papa's face was red also, and I knew he was angry with me. Prince looked at me with disgust as if to say, "I told you not to do that." He gave a snort and trotted back to the barn. Papa said, "In the house with you, after you take that bridle off Prince." For the next two days, you can do Brother's chores for him. Chopping wood, feeding Prince and bringing the eggs from the hen house should keep you out of trouble."

Brother was working hard on a Christmas surprise and I had caused trouble. I decided I would work really hard to do his chores *just right*. At supper that night my misfortune was not spoken of. When Papa asked the blessing at supper, he said he was thankful for his three wonderful children. I was not real sure I should have been included in the blessing part of the prayer. Perhaps Papa should have asked for forgiveness for me instead of a blessing.

Mama and Grandmother were busy baking in the kitchen. Wonderful wisps of fragrances of cinnamon, allspice, apples and cookies filled the house each day, greeting us when we returned from school. Whispers were everywhere. One day I found Grandmother and Mama counting money from the sugar jar. They were whispering about a trip Grandmother and Grandfather would be making to Ironton and about presents. When Grandmother spied me she put her finger to her lips and signaled to Mama to be quiet. "Why son, I thought you and your Brother were in the barn," Mother said. She smiled and winked at Grandmother.

Of course I had my secrets too. I just needed a spot to make my Christmas presents. I was also puzzled about what presents to make. I talked to Mama and she suggested that as I enjoyed writing and drawing, perhaps I could make beautiful Christmas Cards for everyone. I thought about that and decided I would try my hand at art work. I just needed a private spot, a spot all my own. Mama suggested I work in her and Papa's room at the secretary by her and Papa's bed. She said I could pull down the top and no one would ever see what I was working on. The secretary seemed to meet my needs. I pulled the crayons and paper from a drawer, in the little table, by the door in the living room and proceeded to Mama and Papa's room. I labored over my drawings, working until the sun sank below the horizon, for several days. At last I was happy with the results and hid the drawings behind the roll top secretary, ready for Christmas gifts.

I still didn't know what Brother was working on, but all the preparations at school took my mind away from the secrets at home. There was a tree to put up at school and gifts to make for Teacher. I would make a card, wishing Teacher a Merry Christmas. There were decorations to make for our school house. One day we made a red and green paper chain to circle our class-room. How festive we were beginning to look.

Finally the big day arrived at school. The older boys would cut the Christmas tree. Brother had hoped he would be chosen to help select the tree from the woods that surrounded the school. But Teacher chose the oldest of Mont Black's sons, Warren Black. Teacher softened the blow by telling the class Warren would need assistants to help cut the tree and pull it back to the school on the sled. Teacher looked around the classroom and said he would allow Warren's two brothers, Marvin and Victor to go with Warren. I could tell Brother was feeling very sad. Then teacher looked at Brother and said, "I believe they could use one more helper", and he gave Brother the job. Brother hurriedly put on his coat and hat and headed out the door with the three other boys. Warren had brought a sled for pulling the tree back to the schoolhouse and a crosscut saw to cut the tree. We all waited anxiously to see what a beauty of a tree they would bring back to the school, tied to the sled, its branches frosted with snow. Meanwhile, we spent our time cutting paper shapes and coloring them to decorate our tree. Teacher said the girls could pop some pop-corn on the hot pot-bellied heating stove that was fairly dancing, trying to warm the classroom. Our faces turned red from the heat while our backsides were still cold. Sara Black and two other girls helped pop the corn. Teacher said, "You can eat some of the pop- corn, but save enough to trim the tree." Some of the girls had brought needles and thread to string the popcorn. The popped corn was placed in a big bucket and we each took a handful of the popped corn out of the bucket to eat. Meanwhile, the older girls began to pull needle and thread through the white puffs of corn to make a garland to hang on the tree. Betty, one of the bigger girls, let Sister help. I could tell it made Sister feel very grown-up to be using a needle and thread. Sometimes Mama and Grandmother would cut out material and help Sister put in some stitches, making sure the stiches were just right size and evenly placed. I can still hear Grandmother's voice say, "Just a little smaller and keep a fingernail tip space between each stitch, just like this," as she demonstrated the small, precise stitches that Grandmother was recognized for at church quilting bees. Sister was getting the hang of running the needle through the pop-corn, loosing very little of the corn.

We heard a racket in the school yard. We all started for the door, but Teacher called, "Children, move back from the door, I think our tree has arrived. The door was flung open and two of the boys were pulling on the tip of the tree while the other boys were outside, pushing the tree through the door. Along with the tree came a gust of wind and swirling snow. We all shivered as the icy wind wrapped itself along our back- sides, as we hurried to warm ourselves by the stove. "Now, students, move back and let the boys warm up," Teacher said as he gave a shudder himself, chilly from the cold wind. Icy coats and gloves were removed and red hands were held over the stove. Soon it was time for a turn-around as backs needed warmed too.

As the room became more tolerable, our attention turned to the tree. It was an absolute beauty. A deep green coated the needles, the shade of the cedars on Bell Mountain, as the sunset stole the color of the day, turning the trees a deep blue green. Bright blue berries hung thickly on the branches. I thought the tree truly did not need more decorations than nature had already supplied. Teacher had ready the boards and a bucket of sand, ready to stand our tree up at the front of the class-room. The bigger boys helped him stand the tree up amid gasps about its perfection. Soon the tree was covered with popcorn chain and ornaments cut from paper. Then the crowning glory, a star that had been made long ago from tinsel was placed atop the tree. Our room was ready for Christmas, and the Christmas Program.

All the parents would be attending the program, so Teacher said we must know our parts perfectly. We practiced all our songs, *Silent Night, Oh Come All Ye Faithful,* and my favorite, *Rise Up, Shepherd, and Follow.* This was an old spiritual and I liked the rhythm and the way we sang the song with one of the Davis boys singing the lead part and the rest of the students following, with the echo part of the song, *There's a star in the East on Christmas morn,* then we would all sing *rise up shepherd, and follow.* Our singing was much improved due to the singing school, and I thought we sounded as good as the Mormon Tabernacle Choir, which my Mama listened to on the radio. I couldn't wait until the night of our Christmas Program.

Finally the night arrived. Grandmother and Grandfather would take us to the school in their automobile, as Mama did not want Papa riding in the open air of the wagon. All the Mothers had made cookies and we would have hot cocoa to drink, after the program.

Mama fussed with Papa, saying, "Papa, do you think you should be out in the cold?" "Now Mama, I will be just fine." I wouldn't miss my children's Christmas Program for anything. This is Sister's first play. She has worked so hard on the poem she chose to read. I think I know it by heart myself by now. Would you like me to recite it for you?" Mama swatted at Papa and said, "Then be off with you, but you must bundle up."

When Grandfather and Grandmother arrived, Mama had an arm load of blankets to wrap Papa in. Brother carried a box of cookies. We all crowded into Grandfather's little car and down the road we went. "Let's sing some Christmas songs", Grandfather shouted over the auto's motor. "I know, lets sing my favorite Christmas Carol, and then each of you can have a pick." "What is your favorite song Grandfather," I asked? "Why I like *I Saw Three Ships Come Sailing In,*" and with that, Grandfather broke into song and we all joined in. By the time the ship came in with all ten verses, we were at the school, bright with the glow of lamps, shining through the school house windows.

On the school house door hung a wreath made of cedar, bright with holly berries and a red ribbon, on which we had all worked. Inside the school room was the most glorious Christmas tree. Brother had really wanted the honor of cutting down the tree, but that went to the oldest son of Mont Black's Warren. Brother said it was a good choice because he was older and always so helpful to everyone. Colorful paper lanterns swung from string, hanging from the ceiling. I don't believe the brightest lights, which now line the streets of Branson, could ever equal our simple homemade decorations. The smell of the cedar tree filled the school-house.

Sister was to begin the program, as she was the youngest and Teacher was afraid she would be to sleepy to last through the entire program. As excited as she was, I do believe she could have recited her poem at midnight. She stood in front of the classroom and began her poem. "*Once there was a snowman, and continued to tell how this snowman came into the house because he was so cold, but began to melt all over the floor, as he stood by the fire.* Sister had found this poem in a book Aunt had brought her from St Louis last year at Christmas time. The book was well worn by now, as Sister had looked at the beautiful pictures and stories and poems all summer. Several more poems were told and songs were sung, ending with *Silent Night, Holy Night.* I looked at Papa and he had a tear running down his cheek. Mama reached over and patted his hand, I am sure she saw the tears also. The Christmas Program was considered a success. After cookies were served, we loaded into Grandfather's automobile. Mama and Grandfather assisted Papa into the vehicle and Mama fussed and tucked blankets around Papa to ensure he did not take a chill. A soft snow had begun to fall before we reached home.

Papa had leaned back in his seat and was sleeping by the time we pulled into our driveway. Mama gently awakened Papa and pulled his coat collar around his neck. Grandfather helped Papa out and into the house. I could see Mama looked sad, although she praised the program and Sister's reciting of her poem. "Why sister, I don't believe anyone could have done a better job than you did." Grandmother agreed and Sister was full of joy as she climbed the stairs to the room she would share with Grandfather and Grandmother until after Christmas, when they would return to their home.

As soon as the Christmas Program had ended, school was dismissed for the holidays, so we had plenty of time to work on surprises in addition to our regular work. Papa was unable to complete any chores, so most of the farm work fell to Brother and me. There was wood to chop, chickens to tend, a cow to feed and milk. Brother had almost completed the gift he had made, but we were still banned from the shed.

Christmas Eve services were scheduled for the Church, but Mama felt we should celebrate at home this year. After supper was over, Grandfather brought out the big family Bible, reserved for recording the major events of the family's life and for reading on special occasions. Christmas Eve certainly qualified. Grandfather liked to read the Christmas story, starting with Matthew, Chapter I and ending with Chapter III, the return to Nazareth. The lamps had been lit and our small family gathered around Grandfather, as he began to read. I liked the part about the shepherds in the field. I wondered if they had a little mule like Prince, pr0tecting their flocks. After reading the Christmas Story, Grandmother asked Sister to recite her poem again. Sister stood up and recited the poem perfectly. Papa said, "Children, I believe I may have heard the sound of hooves on the roof, the three of you had better scoot off to bed. Saint Nicholas can't slide down the chimney if you are still awake." With that, Sister ran to Mama and Grandfather, Grandmother and Papa, giving them each a hug and kiss. "Oh wait," Mama said, "you haven't hung your stockings yet." Sister raced upstairs and was down in a flash, stocking in hand. Papa had made stocking hangers to go on the mantel years ago. Brother and I brought our stockings and we hung them on the hooks. "Up to bed with all of you," Mama said, "I'll be up to tuck you all in and hear your prayers." Papa no longer climbed the stairs to hear our prayers. We gave him our good-night kisses down stairs. Mama tucked Sister in and came into our room. Brother and me knelt by our beds and asked for blessings on Mama, Papa, Sister and Grandmother and Grandfather. I added a prayer for Prince and all the other animals on Christmas Eve.

Christmas day arrived cold and snowy. The snow was swirling around as Brother and I raced out to feed the animals. We wanted to hurry as Saint Nicholas had arrived, and we were in a rush to see what he had brought us. We took Prince a Christmas carrot and apple from the root cellar and the apple house. The cow was milked and the pigs fed, then we sped inside to find Sister, Mama and Papa and our Grandparents waiting for us. The rule was, on Christmas morning we empty our stockings, before we open our presents. We each found an orange and some nuts along with a red and white candy cane. Hard Christmas candy rounded out the stocking.

Then we gave the gifts we had made. I gave each family member a card. On Grandfather's card, I had drawn a mule, which I thought looked very much like Prince. Grandfather said, "Why I declare son, I believe you have captured the exact likeness of the little mule out there in the barn. How did you get that mule to pose for you long enough for you to draw him?" I flushed with pleasure at Grandfather's praise of my art work. Then I noticed Brother had disappeared. In a moment, I heard knocking at the back door. Mama told me to stay right where I was, she would get the door. Mama came back into the parlor with Brother, and he was carrying the most beautiful red and white sled. This was what he had kept secret from Sister and me. "Can we try it out", I asked? As soon as the rest of the presents are opened and breakfast is finished," Papa said from his chair, which had been pulled up next to the fireplace. Grandmother said, retrieving a package with a red bow from under the tree, "I wonder who this package is for?" It couldn't be for Grace, it's much too big for such a little girl. Why, here it says to Grace, why dear it must be for you," Grandmother said in a shocked voice, handing the gift to Sister. Sister held the package on her lap for a moment before Papa said, "Grace, do we get to see what is in the package?" Sister began tearing at the paper, uncovering a large doll, with blond hair and eyes that opened and closed. "Oh, isn't she beautiful," sister said in a barely audible voice, as she lovingly wrapped her arms around the doll almost as large as she was.

Next it was my turn. I had hoped for a View Master with some slides, but I hadn't dared think I might receive such a coveted present. I slowly opened my package and there it was a View Master Slide viewer, with six sets of slides. I could barely wait for Brother to open his package. As Brother opened his present, an erector set came into view. I knew Brother was very happy with his present, as he enjoyed building things. Mama had knitted hats and gloves for all of us, including Papa and Grandfather. Grandfather had to model his hat for us, assuring Mama it would keep him very warm.

We went into the kitchen to eat breakfast, all declaring it was the very best Christmas ever. After breakfast we all went outside, with the exception of Papa, who watched from his chair at the window. We were a colorful crew, dressed in the hats and mittens and scarves Mama had made us. Greens, blues and reds bobbed up and down the hill as we rode the sled down the hill by the front of the house and pulled it up again. Brother had sanded the runners smooth and the sled fairly flew down the hill.

A bone chilling fog had enveloped our valley by the beginning of January. It seemed to drift down and spread across Bell Mountain and the valley, shortly after New Year's Day and wrap its tentacles of gray ice around our valley and attach itself to all it encountered. Even Prince did not want to leave the shelter of the barn to confront the freezing fog, wafting around the frozen ground and the barren trees.

Papa had seemed to be waiting until Christmas was over to take leave of his little family. He grew weaker with each cold, bleak day of January. At times he would not be able to come to the kitchen to eat breakfast with us. One of us would carry a tray to his bedside and sit with him while he toyed with his food on his plate. Mama made sure he was warm and comfortable. , At the end of the school day we would sit by his bedside, telling him of our day at school, what we had learned and our other adventures. Papa listened intently, not wanting to miss a word of what was happening in our lives. If we did not supply enough information, he would ask questions of each of us. What did we study at school today? What did we do at recess? Sister would recite her spelling words and Papa was so proud when she announced each Friday that she had scored 100 percent on her spelling test. Mama would have to come into the bedroom and tell Papa he needed to rest and we had chores to do before nightfall. Papa reluctantly let us go to do our chores, but only with the promise we would return to talk more after we had finished the egg gathering and the milking and feeding. He always asked about Prince and from time to time we had an escapade to tell Papa about. Papa especially seemed to love to hear stories about Prince.

Papa talked to us about how important we each were to him and Mama. "Boys," he would say, "what a gift God gave me and your Mama when each of you came into our home. Then can you imagine our blessings when Sister arrived. I have had such a blessed life. I could not have asked for more. Even a king on a throne is not as lucky as I am," Papa told us this often. I guess he wanted to make sure we knew how much he loved us.

Papa Has Left Us

On the eleventh of January we returned home from school, riding Prince through the relentless fog and found several buggies and wagons in the yard. Grandfather's auto was parked by the walk. Brother and I slowly walked down the lane, leading Prince with little Sister on his back, not wishing to hurry, dreading the opening of that door. Somehow, we knew when we turned the knob our lives would never again be without an ache inside our hearts. There would always be a longing for Papa. If only we could turn around and ride Prince back to school. If only we didn't have to ride Prince down the lane leading to our front door. I didn't want to move from my position of a spectator of the little clapboard house, with the cars and wagons gathered round. I knew when we walked into our home there was no going back to a time that had been. But as much as I did not want to go forward, an invisible force seemed to be compelling my feet to move and an unseen wind at my back pushed me forward. The three of us stepped upon the painted boards of the porch. Brother slowly raised his hand and opened the door.

Mama was sitting in the hall, waiting for our return. Several women stood around her. It seemed they were nameless and faceless, moving like phantoms in my home. The women parted as we came into the hall. Mama reached out her arms for us, pulling us to her. "Papa had to leave us, his heart was just worn out. Papa loved you all so much." With those words, Brother raced into Papa's room, finding him gone. "Where is Papa, what have you done with him," he cried? We hadn't seen the coffin, sitting in the corner of the parlor. Mama walked with us to look at Papa. He looked so thin, lying so still in his best suit. Two neighbors sat on each side of the coffin. It was the custom for neighbors and family to set with the dead in the home of the deceased. Mama said Papa's funeral would be the next day. Through his tears, Brother said he wanted to be one of the men sitting with Papa all night. Mama started to tell him he was much too young for that duty, but with one look at his face, she hugged him and said, "I think your Papa would be honored." Brother insisted on having Prince pull the wagon caring Papa's body to the church, then to the Ottery Creek Cemetery. Mama said she felt that would be fitting, seeing how Prince had saved our lives last fall.

I heard Brother come up the stairs to put on his work clothes. He tried to be quiet, but I heard him. He looked very tired in the early morning light. He had sat with Papa all night. "Brother," he said, "I'm going out to the barn to brush Prince's hair and make sure he looks proper to carry Papa today." "I'll help," I replied. I had felt so helpless and this was some action that I could be involved in. I had slept very little, but didn't want to disturb the others. I rose in the cold dawn, hurriedly dressing in my old work clothes. As we crept down the stairs, trying not to wake Mama and little sister, we passed the parlor, with Papa lying so still. Mr. Black and Mr. Strickland sat on each side of Papa. I hurried out the door, trying not to look at Papa. I didn't want to think of him lying there, never to put his arm around me or speak to me in his kind voice again. On a day not long before his passing, he had told Brother and me, "Boys, you know your heavenly Father loves you much more than your Mother and I do. He will always listen to your prayers. Don't forget to talk to him." We had told Papa we would remember.

Brother got out the curry comb, while I opened the bin of oats to feed Prince. He seemed to sense our sadness as he nuzzled Brother and then me. After Brother had brushed Prince for a while, I took over, combing Princes tail and mane. He seemed to enjoy all the attention. The cold was creeping inside our jackets, and as much as we dreaded returning to our house, we could not stay in the dreary morning cold any longer.

Brother draped his arm around my shoulder, much like he had when we walked toward our house last summer, talking about Papa's illness. Even with the cold, our steps were slow.

Our home was already filled with our neighbors. Aunt Maude was in the kitchen, whipping up a breakfast for all who were there. Despite our sadness, the cold morning air had brought a hunger to the pit of my stomach, and the smell of Aunt Maude's biscuits, just coming out of the oven, restored my appetite.

"Young men," she called to us, "come and sit down and eat some breakfast. This will be a long day and you need to keep up your strength." Brother and I took our usual seats at the table, Papa's seat remained empty. More friends drifted in and took seats around the table. Uncle asked blessing on all present and especially on Papa's little family. Then the small talk began, talk of the weather, and of crops to be planted come spring.

Try as I might, I don't remember much about that time. I remember Prince pulling the wagon, with Papa's coffin on the back. Mama, Sister and I rode in the car with Grandfather and Grandmother. Brother drove the wagon as he had requested, with Uncle sitting beside him. It was such a gray day and the lamps had to be lit in the church house, even though it was early afternoon. Then the service was over and Papa was placed in the wagon again, for his final journey, up the winding road to the Ottery Creek Cemetery.

When we returned home, the house seemed to still be full of people and there were tables groaning with food, brought by neighbors. I'm not sure when the neighbors began to drift away. It may have been hours or days. A fog seemed to creep into my brain, much like the fog swirling around our valley.

Finally spring arrived and the fog began to lift. We settled into our new life, one without Papa. He was always with us though. I could hear his voice when I had a problem, telling me a story of time when he had encountered a similar incident.

We continued reading the scriptures every night and we said our prayers at bedtime. One night Mama was reading the scripture of our Lord, raising Lazarus from the dead, from the book of John. "Mama," Brother questioned, "if Christ could raise Lazarus from the dead, why couldn't he save Papa?" Brother was crying, his body shaking with despair and doubt. He continued, "one day last winter, as we were returning from school, we saw you and Mrs. Black go into the church. We followed you into the church, but you both were already at the altar, praying for Papa. I thought Papa would be fine. I thought God would hear your prayers and heal Papa. Why didn't he hear you?"

Mama was quite for a moment, I suppose searching for wisdom and the words to answer Brother's doubts. "Yes Son, Golda and I both prayed that day, much like we had done many days before, for your Papa and others. Sometimes we don't understand how

God answers our prayers, but he does hear and he does answer. We just don't always understand. God gave you all a wonderful Father, I think much like our Father in heaven. He taught you how to grow to be kind and good young men and your sister a woman. He taught you lessons that will stay with you in all you may encounter, if you will just think back on what your Papa said and always ask God for his guidance. I wanted so much to keep your Papa here with me and with you children. But our time is not God's time. Today is just a blink in God's eye. Although I don't understand why Papa had to go, I know he taught you children more than many parents teach their children in a lifetime. Your Papa is safe in heaven. No more pain, no sorrow. Someday we will all join him. But for now, we are here to carry out God's plan for our own lives. God did answer my prayers. I just don't have the understanding yet to know how my prayers were answered."

Mama gathered her little brood to her, wrapping her arms around Brother and me as Sister climbed on her lap. We sat there in the lamp glow for a long time. "Just remember what your Papa taught you and always ask God for help," Mama said. "Now it's time for bed. Tomorrow is a school day."

Little Prince stayed and worked with us on the farm during the hard days ahead. Days of the depression, of Papa's death, days of hard, back breaking work for Brother, Mama and me. There were gardens to plant, animals to tend, eggs to gather and sell and firewood to cut. Prince was a faithful part of our family, perhaps sensing how much he was needed.

He never crossed the mountain again. I would like to believe that we always considered what Papa would have said, and to ask for God's blessing in all our growing up. Of course I am sure we failed at times, but Mama and Papa's teaching kept us in good stead.

After Brother and I grew up and left home for work in the city, Mama called and told me that Prince was again running in flower filled meadows, full of timothy grass, a heaven for the long ears to roam. Some of the neighbors buried Prince in the apple orchard. After I retired and moved back to the farm, I at times wander to the orchard and set beside Prince's grave. A few of the rocks still lined his grave when I moved back to the farm. Brother and I replaced some of the missing rocks on a sunny afternoon a few years ago.

As the breeze blows through the trees and bees buzz in the apple blossoms I think of all the days my family and I spent on this little farm in the Ozarks. Now I have Grandchildren with whom I sometimes sit on the front porch and share my stories of Mama and Papa, Grandmother and Grandfather, of wars fought, but most of all the love our family shared. Of course a little mule named Prince left many stories to tell.

CPSIA information can be obtained
at www.ICGtesting.com
Printed in the USA
LVHW090514190419
614798LV00001B/173/P